'So, shall we say many happy returns?'

Guy smiled his slow, easy smile.

'It's the usual thing on a birthday,' Kate said with a laugh. His hand took hers, sending darts of feeling driving through her. 'Still, we'd better get on now, hadn't we?'

'Spoken like a dedicated GP,' he teased. 'See you tomorrow, Cousin Kate,' he said, and then moved away to his own car.

Kate watched him drive off. Cousin Kate, indeed, she thought crossly. He makes me sound like something out of a Jane Austen novel, shawl, bonnet and all!

Janet Ferguson was born at Newmarket, Suffolk, and during her going-out-to-work days was a medical secretary working in hospitals both in London and the provinces. It was when she moved to Saltdean in Sussex that she settled down to writing general fiction novels, then moved on to medical romance. She says, 'As to where I get my ideas for plots (writers are always asked that), they come when I'm walking my dog on the Downs; the wind whispers them into my ear...do this...do that...say this...say that...go home and write it *now*. With the elements that inspire me, not to mention two nurses in my family, I aim to keep writing medical romance, and to "plot till I drop".'

THE LOCUM
AT LARCHWOOD

BY
JANET FERGUSON

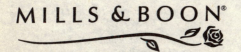

MILLS & BOON®

*First published in Great Britain 1999
Harlequin Mills & Boon Limited,
Eton House, 18-24 Paradise Road, Richmond, Surrey TW9 1SR*

© Janet Ferguson 1999

ISBN 0 263 81522 6

*Set in Times Roman 10½ on 11½ pt.
03-9904-55300-D*

*Printed and bound in Norway
by AIT Trondheim AS, Trondheim*

CHAPTER ONE

THE practice was housed in the annex to Larchwood—Dr John Burnett's home. Set well back from the road in spacious grounds, it was but a stone's throw from the crossroads marking the start of Melbridge, a small but expanding Thames-side town.

There were two partners—John and his niece, Kate Burnett—and up until a fortnight ago, when Dr John had suffered an accident, everything had been going apace, niece and uncle liaising well.

I might have known it couldn't last, Kate was thinking as she stood in the bay window of the second of the two consulting rooms, looking out down the drive.

It was late September, nearly seven in the evening, and the end of a day which had been over-long. Kate was tired, and full of misgivings as well. As from Monday her uncle's stepson, Guy Shearer, would be here as the locum GP, and in no way—none—would he have been Kate's choice.

She parted the slats of the blind and watched the rain as it sheened the laurel hedges, making the sign by the gate—LARCHWOOD HOUSE SURGERY—stand out in clear black and white. Through in the treatment room Sue, the practice nurse, was clearing up after her clinic. This was Friday so only two more days and the black-browed, watchful Guy would be doing his damnedest to boss the show for he was that kind of man.

With her chores done, Sue came through to say good-night. She was Kate's age, nearly twenty-eight and married with two little girls. 'So, what's your step-cousin

5

like?' she asked. 'You've never really said, and as we've got to live with him till New Year I'd like to know what to expect.'

'We-ll...' Kate strained to be fair. 'I hardly know him, Sue. We've only met three times, with the family around as well. I would think, though, that he's the bossy type and likes to do his own thing. He's a big man, striking-looking, burly, with thick dark hair.'

'Sounds like a treat for the patients!'

'True,' Kate forced a smile.

'Where's he been working—I think you said abroad?' Sue reached for her cardigan, buttoning it over her dress.

'In Mtanga, East Africa. He helped set up a clinic there, but he didn't want to sign on for another three years so he's coming home for a time.'

'Is he married?'

'No.'

'Intriguing!' Sue's dark eyes held a glint. 'Anyway, see you *both* on Monday,' she said, and with that and a little laugh she opened the door and ran across the streaming yard to her car.

The taxi that had brought Guy Shearer from the airport had long since left. Kate had glimpsed its roof with the white crest on top slipping between the laurel hedges over two hours ago. She'd imagined the babble of excitement in the house. His mother, Sylvia, would be thrilled to have him home for three months. The fatted calf, in the form of salmon or Dover sole, would be on the table tonight.

I suppose, Kate thought, hesitating before making tracks for home, that I ought to go through to the house and say hello to him. He'll know by my car that I'm still here. It'd look rude to simply drive off.

Going through into the office, she leaned forward towards the mirror and looked anxiously at her face. Now, why hadn't she brought her lipstick and blusher to liven things up a bit? She looked as she felt, which was tired to the bone, which meant plain...plain...plain. Still, there was nothing wrong with her hair—even she could see that. The rich gold of liquid honey, it hung in a chunky bob just above her shoulders, a spiky fringe skimming her brows.

She had been at Larchwood exactly three months, having completed her traineeship with a practice in Wiltshire and passing her MRCGP exam. She could have stayed on with the same practice—the partners had asked her to do so. However, unsettled after Mike, her live-in boyfriend, had gone to work in the States, telling her that he wanted to end their relationship, she'd felt a complete change was due. Mike had been gone just over a year—an unhappy one for Kate—when news came through that her father had died of a heart attack while travelling to his office in Town.

It was when she was home for the funeral that Dr Burnett, with an overload of patients due to new housing in the district, had suggested—had pressed her to join his practice. 'I've got to take in a partner, Katie. I'm rushed off my feet, which isn't fair to my patients or to Sylvia and certainly not to myself.' His brother's death had rocked him. It could easily, he felt, have been him so he'd done his best to persuade her, going on to say, 'Unless you've agreed to stay on at Wiltshire, why not come to me?'

The suggestion had had instant appeal for Kate. It had been time she moved on and forgot the past that contained Mike. She'd been determined to get over him. Not only that, but her mother had needed back-up help for a time so she'd said, 'Yes, please, and thank you for the chance.' The appointment had been sanctioned by the

Health Authority, and Kate had come home to Thames-side.

The accident to her uncle had happened when he'd been driving out to the new housing estate. He'd been hit from behind by a drunken driver and had sustained a whiplash injury, an open fracture of his right arm and three cracked ribs. After a night in hospital he'd been discharged home in a neck collar and a long-arm plaster. His ribs had been left to heal themselves. At first he'd tried to carry on and take his surgeries, but after three days he'd conceded defeat.

Kate had been all set to contact a locum agency in Town when out of the blue Guy Shearer, on one of his transworld phone calls home to his mother, had learned of the accident. As he'd been about to return to the UK he'd suggested that he should speed up the process and help out at Larchwood House.

Relieved beyond measure, John had agreed at once. 'Talk about good luck and timing,' he enthused to Kate. 'I can think of no one I'd rather have to shore us up for a bit. As for Sylvia, she's over the moon. Guy'll live with us here, of course.'

'Of course,' Kate had said, and had wondered why she'd felt so dismayed at the news. After all, she hardly knew the man, having met him only three times.

Still staring unseeingly into the mirror, she thought back over those times. The first had been five years ago when his ex-actress mother, Sylvia, had married Uncle John. The occasion had been a happy one, with Kate's father as best man. Everyone had been glad for John who'd been a widower for ten years, his first wife having died in childbirth along with his baby son.

At the time of the wedding Kate had been in her last year at medical school in Mamesbury in Wiltshire. She had just met Michael Merrow, and had brought him to meet the family, favourably comparing his cool, fair looks with Guy's dark, smouldering ones. Yet even then she'd felt the power of the latter's attraction, had felt a tingling shock when she'd met his eyes which had seemed to run her through. Mike had dubbed him ''strong meat'', which she'd felt to be a fair summing-up.

They'd met again the following year when Guy, practising in Cumbria, had been down for the weekend, his visit having coincided with Kate being home to celebrate passing her finals. As her parents had lived at Grantford, only a mile from Melbridge, there had been a get-together for lunch. Mike had looked interested when Guy had talked of the brain drain and of working abroad.

Kate, on the verge of starting her twelve-month hospital stint, was on cloud nine all that weekend. Mike was a senior physio at the Mamesbury General Hospital and they had just agreed to live together in a tiny flat nearby. He was her first lover and she adored him and the feelings he evoked. Full of the excellent champagne lunch her aunt-in-law provided, she smiled brilliantly over the table at Guy, getting in return a steady amused regard which made her feel foolish and above herself, which perhaps, in part, she was.

A year later he got the Mtanga posting and came south for two nights to say goodbye to his father in London and to John and his mother in Surrey. It was Kate's first week with the Wiltshire practice, but she and Mike managed to make the trip to Melbridge at her uncle's express request. That had been the last time she'd seen Guy. Much had happened since, which wasn't surprising as three years was ages and change was inevitable. Life went on, Kate grimaced at the mirror. What I must do right now is look cheerful and welcoming, and go through to say hello. Picking up her medical case, which rarely left her side, she started to enter the passage which led through into the house when the door at the far end opened and a looming figure emerged. Guy... Well, of course, who else? Kate stiffened and prepared herself. He was in light trousers and a blue shirt and tie, and he was looking straight at her.

'Hello, Kate, it's been a long time.'

'Yes, it certainly has.' She laughed nervously, reacting a little to the touch of his hand, which felt cold as it enclosed hers. Was he missing the African heat already or was jet-lag taking its toll? 'How are you?' she asked, at exactly the moment the same words came from him. She laughed again, but he looked beyond her, saying that he'd come to look around.

'Please,' he added, 'don't let me keep you if you're rushing to get off home.'

He said this as though he didn't want company—or hers at any rate. Well, if that was the case, tough, she thought. She meant to show him around in the way a partner would show a *locum* around for that was what he was. He tried to pass her, but she turned and kept level, telling him that she wasn't in any special hurry and would he please come through? Not that she needed to have bothered for he was already there, in Reception, looking over the counter into the waiting area.

He took his time, his eye moving over the rows of grey plastic chairs, the jumble of children's toys in one corner and the curling magazines, not to mention the pinned-up notices about flu jabs and prescriptions, special clinics and home visits and polite requests not to smoke.

'Must have been difficult for you, coping on your own,' he remarked as they moved from room to room. She told him that her uncle had given much support behind the scenes.

'It didn't do for him to show himself, though. He looked worse than the patients. It's so good that you've come.' She strained to be generous but got little response from the man at her side, who went on to ask what staff were employed. 'We have two receptionists and a senior secretary who manages the practice. We have a nurse who has a clinic here three days a week. We share the district nurse team with two other practices and a health visitor calls each day, but I expect Uncle has told you that already,' she added pointedly, for his attention seemed to be wandering. What an offhand man he was. Even so, she ploughed on, determined to do the right thing. She was the one he'd be working alongside so she must make sure he knew the full drill.

'You'll remember the two consulting rooms...' She led the way into hers. 'The larger one across the passage is Uncle's—yours, of course, as from Monday onwards as you're taking over his list.'

'Quite,' Guy said, so quietly that she wasn't sure if he'd spoken at all. Standing there with his hands on his hips, he was making an assessment of the room, taking in the stripped couch, the big leather-topped desk, the washbasin, filing cabinets and the block of forms under a weight.

'We're not into computers yet, but I mean to press for them. I expect you're thinking that we're way behind the times.'

'Believe you me...' he dropped into Dr John's swivel chair '...this is the acme of comfort and modernity after conditions in Africa.' He leaned back, his arms on the chair arms and his legs a little apart. As he looked like staying there Kate sat as well—on the patient's hard-backed chair at the side of the desk. Facing him in this rather better light afforded by the bay window, she was shocked to see how tired he looked. Deep furrowed lines ran down each side of his nose, while his mouth was set tight.

Concern made her ask, 'Shouldn't you be resting?'

'You mean, after the flight?' Two well-defined brows rose.

'That's exactly what I mean.' She met his eyes squarely, refusing to be put down.

'Later will do,' he said testily, and in the next breath asked after her mother. 'I was sorry to hear about Mr Burnett. It must have been a terrible shock.'

'It was, and thank you for writing.' His letter had been kind, addressed jointly to her mother and herself. She could remember the wording well. 'Mother's fine,' she told him. 'She keeps busy and involved with her pet rescue work. At the moment we're fostering an elderly collie with tunnel vision and a snappy little terrier who keeps making grabs for our heels.'

'Terriers love heels.' When he smiled he looked different. The lines on his face bent the other way—outwards in curving brackets instead of hanging down straight. 'Was your father's death the reason you came home to live or were there other considerations?' he asked her next.

Kate's heart beat hard while her mouth ran dry. Don't let him ask about Mike, don't let him ask about Mike, she prayed, or I might make a fool of myself. 'There was the lure of a partnership, wasn't there? I didn't think twice about it.' Now her smile was forced and brilliant, giving him the false impression that she was mightily pleased with herself.

'Don't the patients get confused with two Doctors Burnett at their disposal?' he enquired, leaning forward in the chair. There was a hint of a taunt in his tone and attitude, which wasn't lost on Kate.

'We're referred to as ''Dr John'' and ''Dr Kate'',' she

informed him crisply. 'To date there's never been any confusion, and now, of course, with Uncle out of action and you in his place, all will be crystal clear. No names could be more different than Shearer and Burnett.'

'True.' He was managing to look bored now. Well, so be it. Kate got to her feet. She'd gone through the motions and been dutifully welcoming—the rest could wait until next week. She was aware of him rising. He'd plainly forgotten that the chair was a swivel one, and heavy and cumbersome into the bargain, for as his weight left the seat the chair swung round and thwacked against his thigh.

Expecting him to curse, she was startled when he grunted with pain and sat again, all but slumping. Sweat started out on his face. 'Guy, what is it? Did you catch a nerve? That chair can be devilish.' She moved to his side as he shook his head, puffing out his breath. Her thoughts rioted. He was ill—that was obvious. He'd brought something back with him, some ghastly bug...malaria, dengue, yellow fever perhaps. Another invalid was all she needed. So much for him being a help.

'No need to write me off so soon!' He was getting to his feet, but more warily this time, ignoring her helping hand.

'It's jet-lag, is it?' She stepped back from him.

'It's a slit in my thigh.'

'A slit in— What did you say?' She stared at him, her hazel eyes wide.

'A slit in my thigh.'

'You mean, a wound?'

'That's exactly what I mean.'

'How did you get it?' Her eyes moved to his lap, then back again to his face.

'I got in the way of a flick-knife at the airport. Some

hyped-up lunatic youth went on a stabbing spree soon after we'd passed through Customs. He was caught and marched off, but not before several passengers, including a child, had been hurt. All I caught was a glancing blow, not a stab as such. I was patched up at the medical centre, along with the others—apart from the child, who was a hospital case. The mother was distraught.'

'Good Lord, how *awful*!' Kate's expression was horrified.

'All I needed was four stitches. In fact, I felt the wound was slight enough to be drawn together with Steristrips. However, I bowed to the judgment of the MO who, incidentally, turned out to be an erstwhile colleague from my medical school days. He directed me to the hotel where I changed out of my suit and cleaned up, which is why I was late. I should have been at Larchwood soon after lunch.'

Kate was still aghast. 'Whatever did Uncle and Sylvia say? I mean, they must have been absolutely—'

'They don't know about it.'

'But, Guy…'

'I didn't tell them, and I don't want you to.' His eyes held hers steadily.

'But that's crazy!'

'On the contrary, it's sensible. If John knew he'd insist that I was unfit to practise next week. Ma would freak out, and the whole thing would be blown up to daft proportions. All I've got is a nick, which will heal in a matter of days provided, of course, I keep out of the way of chairs with a life of their own!'

'I think you should tell someone other than me,' Kate said firmly, and was about to touch on the possibility of infection when Dr John came in.

'Been giving him his orders, Kate?' His uninjured arm came to rest about her shoulders. 'Good to see him, isn't it? Now, why don't you come through and have supper with us, my dear? Sylvia's sent me to tell you it's ready.'

'I'd love to,' Kate replied, not altogether truthfully, 'but my own meal will be waiting for me. Mother's pretty long-suffering, but she doesn't like wasting food.'

'Course not, and quite right, too,' Dr John said at once. 'We just wondered, though, if she might be out, letting canines off chains!'

Kate laughed. 'I hope not.' She picked up her case. 'We're full up as it is.' Then, not trusting herself to say any more or look in Guy's direction, she mumbled good-night and slipped away, running through the now fast-falling rain to her red Volvo.

The feeling of incredulity was still with her as she got in and switched on. What a thing to happen to him within minutes of touching down. Fancy braving all the hazards of Africa only to get knifed over here. She had a strong feeling, too, that he hadn't told her *all* that had happened.

I should have alerted Uncle just now, she thought. He and Sylvia ought to know about it. I didn't actually promise I wouldn't say anything so it's really up to me. I could ring them up later this evening, but on the other hand he told me in confidence, didn't he? Although he wouldn't have done that if the chair hadn't given the game away.

Uncertain what to do for the best, she argued with herself all the way to Grantford and all the way over the bridge that spanned the river at Challoners Corner. She was still in a state of flux when she turned into the drive of Riverstone Lodge a few minutes later.

'I thought you were never coming,' Laura Burnett called out from the porch. 'I suppose you got caught up with Guy's arrival, did you?' Sandy-haired and plump in a green dress with slimming stripes, she scooped up Sparky, the terrier, as Kate garaged the car.

'Yes, he wanted to look round and I couldn't rush off. You know how it is,' Kate said, reappearing and making a dash for the porch.

'How did he look? Has he changed much?' Laura enquired. She liked Guy, Kate remembered, and so had her father, come to that.

'He's thinner, I think, but otherwise the same.' Kate went towards the stairs. 'I'll have a quick shower and be down in seconds,' she called back to her mother, climbing away from any more questions about Guy.

'There was some sort of incident at the airport today—it was on the news,' Laura went on. 'I couldn't hear properly, I was through in the kitchen, but I think it said something about people being taken to hospital…about people being hurt. I don't suppose Guy saw anything of it, did he? Of course, North Row is a very big place.'

Kate was saved from replying, and perhaps from lying, by the chirp of the telephone. Through the bannister staves she could see her mother going to answer it. She heard her say, 'Yes, yes, what's up?' Then came a scandalised, '*No!*' After a pause she went on, 'Clare, with the best will in the world, love, I truly can't tonight. Seven is more than I can handle, and it wouldn't be fair to Kate. She needs her rest, and at that age they'll be squealing half the night.'

Sounds like a litter of pups to house, Kate thought to herself, going into her bedroom and stripping off her workaday skirt and blouse. As she stood under the shower, feeling some of the tension ease from her body, she debated on what she'd say if her mother mentioned Guy and the airport again.

As it happened, she didn't. All the time they were

eating their lamb chops and calabrese she was full of the news that a box of pups had been dumped near Challoners Bridge. 'Seven of them, Kate, and Clare thinks they're only about a month old. She's taking them to the Milland Animal Sanctuary, at least for tonight. I didn't think we could have them, not with Merle and Sparky as well.'

'Quite right,' Kate said absent-mindedly. She was thinking of Guy again. It was possible, in fact likely, she thought, that the airport incident would be reported on *News at Ten,* which she meant to watch. Luck was on her side for at a quarter to ten Laura went upstairs for a bath.

And it *was* on. It came second to an account of a rail accident in India. First there was the newsreader's announcement. Kate glued her eyes to his face, all but lipreading his words, anxious not to miss a single one.

'There was a stabbing incident at Terminal Seven, North Row, at lunchtime today. A white youth, brandishing a flick-knife, injured several passengers, one of them a child, in the main arrivals hall. Further casualties were prevented by the swift action of a passenger off the East African flight, who grappled with the youth, managing to hold him until Security took over.'

Then came film, showing the crowd scattering as the youth lunged, and the figure of a man—*not just a man, but Guy*—struggling with the boy, knocking his arm up, knocking the knife from his hand, fighting to hold him, keeping him pinioned until the airport police rushed to the scene.

Kate cried out—she couldn't help it. She felt cold and all but missed the newsreader's final words. 'Was taken into custody and will appear before the Magistrate's Court tomorrow.'

Flushed now, and in a flurry of excitement, she leapt

to her feet. Why hadn't Guy explained...? Why hide a thing like that? Unable to contain herself any longer, she tore up the stairs to Laura who, in an old dressing-gown which had belonged to her husband, was towelling her short hair. 'I've just seen the news.' Kate sat on the bed. 'It had that airport thing on again.'

Alerted by the throb in Kate's voice, Laura turned on the stool. 'What was it, a bomb?'

'No, a boy with a knife!' Out came the whole story— how Guy had been involved, how he'd been hurt, how he'd bound her to secrecy. 'There he was, plain as plain on the screen, Mummy, and he didn't say a word—not one word about that, nothing about tackling the youth. Talk about hiding your light under a bushel!'

'Well, he won't,' Laura said, only marginally less traumatised than her daughter, 'be able to hide it much longer, will he? John and Sylvia watch *News at Ten* every single night.'

'Yes, I know.'

'And Sylvia will go berserk.'

'I know that too, and a great big fuss and hassle is the last thing Guy wants.'

'I suppose it's just possible,' Laura said more thoughtfully, brushing her damp hair down flat, 'that as Guy's home they may forget to switch on tonight. They'll have lots to talk about, won't they? On the other hand, to-morrow's papers—'

'I hope Uncle finds out tonight,' Kate broke in. 'If something should go wrong with that leg... The knife was probably filthy, and even if Guy's had an antibiotic things could still go wrong.'

'Now *you're* fussing,' Laura said accusingly. 'Guy's a grown man and a doctor to boot. He'll know all the hazards. If his leg starts acting up he'll know what to do.'

'I suppose so.' Kate was unconvinced.

'And what *you* should do,' her mother urged, 'is have an early night. You've had a rough fortnight and you're worn out. You're not on call, I hope?'

'No, the Grainger practice is standing in for us.'

'Well, then?' Laura pressed.

'OK, OK, I'll do as you say.' It was easier to give in than argue so Kate hit the sack early that night.

She couldn't relax, though, not for a long time. When sleep eventually came so did the dreams that rode in on the back of her daytime thoughts—dreams about Guy's leg going septic, about him becoming suddenly ill, so ill that he couldn't summon help, about her uncle pointing an accusing finger and shouting, 'Kate, this is all down to you!'

CHAPTER TWO

IT WAS annoying for Kate to wake up next morning with Guy still on her mind. She must find out exactly how he was, either directly or by devious means. While she was dressing, pulling on leggings and a big white overshirt, she debated how best to contact him without seeming too concerned.

'I thought,' she said to her mother over breakfast, 'that I'd run into Melbridge this morning. I promised Uncle I'd try to get him Robert Goddard's latest book. If Marrisons have got it I could drop it off at Larchwood on my way home.'

'And see how the land lies apropos, Guy?' Laura nodded approvingly. 'If you like, I'll come too,' she added, spreading unsaturated margarine over her toast. 'I'd like to see Guy, not to mention John. I've not been over for a week. There are one or two things I need to do first, though. Perhaps we could leave about ten.'

'Suits me.' Kate looked at the clock—two more hours to go. She decided to pass them by raking up leaves at the top of the orchard. Going out there half an hour later she could feel the sun warm on her back, but the wind was cool. Summer had gone away for another year.

In four days they'd be into October, and a week after that she would be twenty-eight, only two years off thirty—a truly sobering thought. It wouldn't, she realised, have been quite so sobering if she'd still got Mike. 'I always felt he'd be there for me,' she said out loud, drawing the pile of sodden leaves into a sausage-shaped heap.

The sound of a car door closing made her glance towards the house. Her uncle's black Rover stood at the gate, and striding round its front, his dark head erect as he looked about him, was Guy in a light grey suit. He bent to the passenger door to help her uncle out. Kate drew in her breath. He must be all right. Why on earth had she bothered to worry? Not that it had been anything but professional concern, of course.

Her mother had seen them and, preceded by the dogs, both in full bark, she was hurrying to greet them. Her cropped hair moving up and down like a lid.

Watching the little tableau from behind the screen of trees, Kate saw her mother embrace Uncle John, then shake Guy's hand. Setting down her rake, she went to join them, feeling, unusually for her, self-conscious, even wary. Did Uncle John know about Guy?

'My cover's been blown,' Guy informed her, as they went into the house and through into the conservatory, where the sun poured a welcome warmth.

'And not before time!' Dr John exploded. 'What a thing to keep quiet about! He didn't intend to tell us, Katie, and presumably neither did you!'

'Well, as to that—' Kate avoided Guy's eye '—I hadn't firmly made up my mind. As it happened, things were decided for me. I expect you saw the news?'

'We did,' both men said in unison.

Dr John went on. 'The papers had the story this morning—both the *Telegraph* and the *Mail*.'

Guy's chin jerked and he looked irritated, 'Chris Jaley, my MO friend at the airport, must have given out details,' he said.

'You were brave.' Laura appeared with a tray, which Guy took before Kate could get up.

'It was one of those occasions,' he explained, 'when

you act without thought. There was no time for that so bravery didn't come into it.'

'Then we'll have to agree to differ.' Laura handed him his coffee, urging him to help himself to biscuits and passing the sugar bowl. He took both, Kate noticed, and these small indulgences had the effect of making him seem less high and mighty, more on a level with her.

She noticed other things, too, like the movement of his shoulders under his well-cut jacket, the way his hair was thick and capped his head with a tendency to wave at the nape. She also noticed the shape of his hands and his short blunt nails, his wrists brown against spanking white cuffs. Her eyes flicked downwards. Did his leg pain him? He gave out no signs that it did, but his trousers were the easy-fitting kind, lacking the tight clutch of jeans.

Looking up, she encountered his steady gaze—that amused gaze of his that she remembered from four years ago when they'd all been at Larchwood for lunch. It was a shock to realise how well she remembered him but, then, he's not, she thought as she sneaked a glance at his profile, the sort of man you can dismiss from your mind, even if you want to. He sticks in it like superglue.

'We're out, touring the district.' Dr John moved his neck carefully within the confines of his collar as he sipped his coffee. 'I wanted to point out the best routes for Guy when he's making his house calls. We haven't got very far as yet, though. We weakened and called in here.'

'How sensible,' Laura said warmly, lifting Sparky onto her lap.

The doctor went on. 'I'm not very comfortable riding in a car at the moment so I wondered...' he looked at Kate, who guessed what was coming '...if you could spare an hour, my dear, to drive around with Guy while

I stay here and talk to your mother. How's that for an idea?'

'Scarcely a good one, from Kate's point of view.' Guy's cup went down with a bump. 'I have a map, John, and I can read it. There's no reason at all why Kate should give up her morning.' His eyes challenged Dr John's.

There was a second or two when no one said anything, then Kate weighed in. 'I was going into Melbridge this morning anyway. A lift in the Rover would be helpful, and I could point out landmarks on the way. We have quite a few patients this side of the river, although most are in Melbridge, of course.'

'In that case, I'll take you in,' Guy said flatly, leaving Kate with the feeling that he'd somehow turned the tables. But surely it was she who was conveying the favour, not the other way round.

This so rankled that a few minutes later, as they drove off down Guessens Road, she pointed out that her uncle was inclined to harness people together and expect them to be pleased. 'You won't be saddled with me beyond Melbridge, though. I've a fair bit of shopping to do, and these things take time.'

'How much time?' Without turning her head, she saw his hand twitch on the wheel.

'Well, about... I should think at least an hour.'

'Then I'll pick you up on my way back.'

'You don't have to do that. I can get the bus.'

'Yes, I dare say you can,' he said. After that she didn't know what to suppose or what he intended. What a maddening man he was. Plainly the next three months were going to be difficult ones.

They began the run into Grantford with its Saturday traffic. Trying to hide her discomfiture, Kate began to talk very fast. She mentioned that her mother and uncle would be glad of the chance to chat. 'They'll probably natter on about Dad all the time until we get back.'

'They were alike, weren't they—the two brothers?' Guy was looking ahead at a green bus which was about to stop and disgorge its passengers.

'In looks, yes, but otherwise not,' Kate was careful to explain. 'Dad was a worrier and kept things to himself, whereas Uncle John explodes at the least thing and gets it all off his chest.'

Guy nodded, but made no comment. Grantford swirled past—the crowds, the shops, the open market, the town hall with its Gothic front. Soon they'd be through it. Feeling that they couldn't sit in silence, Kate ventured to say that Larchwood had several patients on its northern side. 'Most of this area, though…' she cleared her throat '…is covered by the Grainger practice. It's they who occasionally stand in for us at weekends.'

'Like this one.' Guy braked at the lights. Kate felt him glance at her.

'Yes, and, of course, we'd reciprocate if necessary.' She swallowed and went on doggedly, 'But as they're a three-doctor practice they work out their weekends among themselves.'

'Quite so,' Guy commented.

They left Grantford behind. Next stop Melbridge. They were approaching the bridge at speed. Soon they'd be over it and down on the southern side. The river drowsed in the autumn sunshine. Further along by the trees two schoolboy anglers were casting their lines and a girl was pushing a buggy along the towpath, her hair streaming out behind.

Running out of things to say, Kate was relieved when the Melbridge war memorial could be seen at the head of the town. 'Look, Guy, why not set me down here?'

she said all in a rush. 'Once we're into the town centre stopping will be that much more difficult.'

'Oh… Right… Just as you like.' He sounded uncertain. Was he, Kate wondered, having second thoughts? Was he after all going to suggest that she stayed with him till he'd completed his tour, and deal with her shopping on the way back? No, he was slowing, preparing to stop. He pulled to the side of the road and she undid her seat belt, bending her head to the task.

'I'll be back here in roughly an hour to pick you up,' he said. This time she didn't argue. She looped her bag over her shoulder and fumbled with the doorcatch.

'Here, let me.' Guy leaned across her to open the door. Just for a second the clean male scent of him was all about her, and she found herself holding her breath.

'Thanks,' she said briefly as she got out, all but falling onto the kerb. 'Hope you get on all right. See you here in an hour.'

As the car drew away Kate's composure returned, along with her bated breath. He was attractive-plus, especially close to. Why, she'd almost felt magnetised, wanting to touch him and have him touch her. What a state to be in, she thought. Of course, at the moment I'm sex-starved so why am I so surprised? I'm good at diagnosis, aren't I? Physician, heal thyself. I can't, though, not without Mike. It's Mike I still love and want.

She thought of him as she did her shopping, diving into Smiths and out again and into Marrisons to look for her uncle's book. Mike dogged her steps and filled her thoughts. He was the cause of a raw loneliness that gripped her as she mingled with the crowds, singling out couples on the escalator, going up to the restaurant. What would be the time now in Boston, Massachusetts? She tried to work it out. What were he and Caro Ellenburgh doing at this moment—the bewitching Caro with her big glasses and her glossy hair and mouth full of perfect teeth?

After the book was found and purchased and she'd had a desultory look at clothes, Kate walked through the park to the memorial. She spotted the car already there, parked under some trees, and as she drew nearer she could see Guy, poring over a map spread on the steering-wheel. He folded it and put it away when he saw her appear at the side of the car. 'All done, then?' He smiled at her.

He seemed to be in a rather different frame of mind, more disposed to be friendly, she thought. Maybe, while he'd been driving around, he'd decided that even though they were by no means two of a kind they could put on a reasonable front. On the other hand, it could just be that his leg had stopped hurting. No one in pain, how-ever slight, was ever at their best.

'Yes, I got what I wanted,' she told him as she climbed in and watched him start the car. 'How did you get on?'

'Area sussed out. Every road and ditch conveyed to memory.' He laughed.

'Good,' Kate said, catching his mood and feeling—if only for the moment—more at home with him. She felt bold enough to enquire about his leg.

'Oh, pretty good.' He let in the clutch and the car moved smoothly off. 'It's stopped throbbing. It wasn't deep, you know. It was that child who came off the worst. As a matter of fact I rang Leddingham Hospital while you were shopping—that's where she was taken—and they told me she'd been discharged.'

'Oh, well, that's a relief.'

'Certainly is.'

'What will happen to the youth who did it?'

Guy shrugged. 'I wouldn't like to predict. I just hope

he won't be bailed and let out to do more damage. What do you do with yourself at weekends, Kate?' He changed the subject so abruptly that Kate had a job to click her mind back into place.

'I haven't had all that many off yet,' she said with a little laugh, 'but I belong to the leisure complex out at Barham Rise. There are squash courts there and swimming, ten-pin bowling and aerobics, not to mention an ice rink just under construction. Barham is six miles north of here so it's not too far to go. That's where the new health centre is. Uncle's probably told you about it.'

Guy nodded, but made no comment as he breasted the bridge. He turned his sun-flap down, then commented that he was off to London that afternoon to see his father.

'He'll be thrilled to see you, no doubt,' Kate said.

'And I to see him.' He half smiled, picking up speed once they were back on the flat.

Kate knew a little about Marcus Shearer. He was managing director of a publishing house in Red Square; he lived at Hampstead and hadn't remarried since he and Sylvia divorced eight years ago. Guy would have been twenty-six then, most likely doing his year on the wards at the Walbrook where he had trained. 'Will you drive up?' she asked him.

'No, go by rail, I think. Save my strength for Monday!' He flung her a quick amused glance.

'How sensible,' Kate replied, in unwitting parody of her mother. 'Monday surgeries in England, as I'm sure you remember, are the busiest of the week.'

One working week later it was plain to everyone that Guy had forgotten little or nothing about practising medicine in the UK. He filled his stepfather's place with confidence and energy, but without the bombast Kate had feared. The staff were all over him, but she'd expected that. What was important was that the patients he saw went away feeling, as they always did with her uncle, that they were in caring and competent hands.

The eighth of October was Kate's birthday, a day that started out much the same as any other, with the staff preparing for morning surgery while the first booked-in patients gathered on the pavement outside. Sue was in the office, checking her appointments with Janice, the office manager. Guy was in his room just across the passage, busy opening his mail. Kate could hear the faint sound his paperknife made as he slit the envelopes.

He had brought her the latest Joanna Trollope for her birthday—the hardback, which was a generous present. She'd already thanked him for it. Her uncle's and Sylvia's gift was a soft-as-butter leather shoulder-bag in a subtle shade of cream. The staff had given her cards and serenaded her at her desk. Back home there were other gifts and cards.

Nothing from Mike. Not that she'd expected there would be, but had he, she wondered, remembered what day it was and spared her a fleeting thought? His defection, or rejection of her, still caused her anguish at unguarded moments. The hurt went very deep. It seemed strange to think she'd never see him again, never again know the joy of holding him and having him hold her... It was like saying goodbye to a life.

Guy's buzzer, summoning his first patient, jerked her into action. Her first patient this morning was a young mother, bringing in her toddler for an MMR injection. Emily was two, and gave a piercing shriek as the needle went into her thigh. She rubbed the spot of her own accord, pouting balefully at Kate. 'Her daddy didn't want her done at first,' the mother said. 'He doesn't believe in triple injections, but I persuaded him in the end.'

'Measles, especially, is a very nasty illness with unpleasant side-effects,' Kate said, as she marked the little one's vaccination card. 'Emily may get a slight reaction in about a week's time—something resembling a slight cold—but it shouldn't bother her.'

'Hope not, otherwise Ken will go on something alarming,' Rose Challis said, gathering up her now calm infant, and going out of the door.

Then Kate saw a teenage boy with acne, followed by a bronchitic grandpa, brought in by his daughter who said that he kept the whole family awake, coughing in the night. A menopausal lady came next and after her a man of fifty, who was suffering anxiety and stress following the death of his wife. Kate spent more than the usual six minutes talking to him. She was unwilling to prescribe antidepressant tablets until she had seen him again.

When the last patient had been seen and the street door was closed, the clerical side sprang into action. The morning mail was dealt with, referral letters were written to consultants, forms for special tests were made out and a number of phone calls were made. Guy and Kate conferred about a patient with ME and Sue came through with a tray of blood and urine specimens for sending to the hospital labs.

At half past eleven Guy and Kate usually set off on their home visits, but this morning they were due at the Melbridge Nursing and Residential Home to give the influenza vaccine to any patients who wanted it. They went in separate cars, Guy's following Kate's onto the nursing home forecourt.

They were met by the matron, a young woman in her thirties, who looked harassed and hot. Removing her misted-up spectacles and thrusting back her hair, she offered them coffee, which Guy refused quickly before

Kate could speak. 'I'll take the bed patients in the nursing wing, Kate,' he said, without looking at her. 'You do the ambulant ones. I'll see you down here later on.'

He had his bossy boots on this morning, Kate thought, as a staff nurse came to assist her while Guy, accompanied by Matron Carr, strode towards the lift.

The elderly residents were all over the place—in the corridor on sticks or Zimmer frames or shuffling along by the walls. Some were in the big lounge, watching television, some in their separate rooms. They all looked well cared for, but most were sad-faced and many didn't care whether they had the vaccine or not, although they duly presented an arm or a shoulder, suitably bared by the nurse. Kate felt she'd never come to the end of them all, and was relieved when Guy—sans matron, who'd been called to the phone—came to help her out.

There was a noticeable brightening-up all round when he came into the lounge. He was asked by one old lady if he was new. 'It's a treat to see a man with nothing wrong with him—they're all old crocks in here.'

Another old lady, who'd had a leg amputated due to ischaemia, asked him if she'd grow another one 'because I'm quite healthy otherwise.' Guy's reply was that he didn't think it was likely, but he felt that as she was managing so well with just one it might not matter too much. She was plainly gratified by this, agreeing at once to have her flu jab. 'Because you've been kind and I like to oblige when I can.'

One of those who refused it was the oldest patient in the home. She was a hundred and two and knew her own mind. 'No, thank you, Doctor,' she said. 'I've done very well without it so far so why rock the boat?'

'Well, that was an edifying experience,' commented Guy as, once more escorted by matron, he and Kate prepared to leave. He didn't laugh as he said it, though.

In fact, thought Kate, he looked thoughtful, even gloomy. Maybe he was envisaging himself in his eighties and beyond, and not liking what he saw. 'Are you making any calls before lunch?' he asked Kate as she prepared to slip into her car.

She told him she wasn't. 'It's too late now. I'll drive home to lunch then start again afterwards. I've nothing urgent until two.'

'Neither have I.' There was a pause, then Guy said, 'How about us having lunch together?'

'You mean, out somewhere?' Kate couldn't quite manage to keep the surprise from her voice for there had been no kind of socialising since Guy started. He lunched at Larchwood and Kate back home at Riverstone Lodge, they took turns to take evening surgery. They were a bit like Box and Cox, a state of affairs which suited Kate perfectly, but now...

'Yes,' he said, 'I do mean out somewhere.' Guy moved back to let a small B.T. van park by the opposite wall.

'Because it's my birthday, I suppose?' she suggested, a little ungraciously.

'If you want a reason, yes.' He looked at her directly, the sun full on his face. 'We could go to the Melbridge Arms, have a drink at the bar, then wend our way through into their restaurant section for whatever's on offer. I went there the other evening and found it excellent.'

'Thank you, I'd like that. It's kind of you, Guy.' She remembered her manners at last.

'I'm a kind man,' he jested, which made her laugh and also put paid to the faint embarrassment which had been making her sound like a schoolgirl on her first date.

The Rover was parked in front of her Volvo so she followed it onto the road, down the hill and left to the hotel. It was a sparkling October day, and for the first time since she'd got up she felt her spirits lift. She also felt hungry, and thoughts of Mike took themselves off.

He came into the conversation, however, some twenty minutes later when over the melt-in-the-mouth steak and kidney pie, a speciality of the house, Guy asked, quite casually, 'So, what happened to Mike Merrow?'

A pang shot through Kate. It was a question she'd hoped he'd never ask, but now that he had she must lie a little or leave the worst out, as she had with everyone else. No one, except her mother, knew the painful truth. 'He got a job in Boston so off he went,' she said carefully, not overdoing the brightness but hoping she'd got it just right.

'And you didn't want to go with him?'

'No.' This time she managed to smile in the face of the lie she was telling. 'I didn't want to work over there.'

'I seem to remember that you knew one another for a very long time.' He raised his glass and drank deeply, not looking directly at her.

'We lived together for two and a half years but we knew each other for a year before that so, yes, a long time.'

'As long as some marriages last these days.'

'What a cynical remark, Dr Shearer!' she bantered desperately, relieved beyond measure when he changed the subject to his father.

'He's getting married again, would you believe? Gave me quite a shock. He's marrying one of his writers. The wedding is next month.' Now Guy was smiling straight at her.

'I can see you're pleased,' she said.

'Delighted—couldn't be more so. They've known one another some time. Jean is a crime novelist, same age as Pa, writes under the name of C.P. Shaw. She's not a best seller, but she does all right and is a very interesting woman. Pa and Ma were divorced eight years ago so no one could say he's rushed into matrimony again. He's like me—a wary old bird.'

Kate digested this. 'Does your mother...does Sylvia know?' she asked.

'She does and, though amazed, says she's glad it's Jean. The two of them met at a literary party before the marital split. Funny how things turn out, isn't it? I suppose you could say that life has some sort of pattern to it—when viewed from hindsight, that is.'

Kate nodded, although unconvinced, and their talk moved on to books and thence to films and television and the parts Guy's mother had played. 'She was superb in that medical drama that used to run on Saturday nights. Would she take a part now, do you think, if she was offered a suitable one?' Kate asked. She sometimes thought that Sylvia hadn't enough to do, which meant that she concerned herself too much with other people's affairs.

'No, she's adamant that she won't. She says this time she's making marriage a full-time commitment. I dare say she's wise. At close on sixty there aren't all that many lead parts. She acts enough in real life, anyway!' Guy said this unsneeringly but with a hint of annoyance. 'She's telling half the population of Melbridge about her heroic son!'

'Oh, you mean the airport accident? Well, you did jump to it, Guy. Act swiftly, I mean, without thought for yourself,' Kate said quietly. There was no reply from the man at her side. Kate glanced down at his thigh. Dr Grainger, over at Grantford, had seen to the removal of his sutures. Guy had registered with him as a temporary resident at her uncle's suggestion for to be treated by a GP who wasn't a relative was usually the wisest thing.

Sue, though, had been sorely disappointed at not having him under her wing. 'Taking out his stitches would have been a perk,' she'd declared. 'I'd have hung them round my neck in a locket... They'll be wasted on the Grainger lot!'

'So, what are you doing to celebrate your birthday?' he asked her next.

'Not a lot, but I'm going out this evening with three friends,' she said. Deliberately she didn't explain that they were all female, that they were having a girls' night out. If he liked to think it was the usual mixed set four-some, so much the better. She didn't want any more probing into her personal life, nor did she want him to think that she couldn't summon up a male companion when the occasion warranted it.

Out in the yard, under the trees where they'd left their cars, she thanked him for the lunch. 'I enjoyed it,' she said to the back of his jacket as he bent to unlock her door.

'I, too.' He handed her the keys, dropping them into her palm then closing her fingers over them, and looked down at her from under his brows. 'So, shall we say many happy returns?' He smiled his slow, easy smile.

'It's the usual thing on a birthday,' Kate said with a laugh, choosing to ignore his meaning. His hand took hers, sending darts of feeling driving through her. 'Still, we'd better get on now, hadn't we?' She removed her hand from his.

'Spoken like a dedicated GP,' he teased. 'Have a good time tonight. We all need fun in our lives. Far better that than all pills we're so good at prescribing. See you to-morrow, Cousin Kate.' He moved away to his own car, turning to wave before he stepped inside.

Kate watched him drive off and waited until the

Rover's sleek chassis was out on the road and out of sight, before setting off herself. Cousin Kate, indeed, she thought crossly. He makes me sound like something out of a Jane Austen novel, shawl, bonnet and all.

CHAPTER THREE

NEXT morning's surgery started much as usual, but failed to go on that way. Shortly before ten a.m., while Kate was examining a patient, she became aware of a disturbance in the waiting-room where a child was yelling full blast. Expecting the noise to cease, for surely the mother wouldn't let it go on, she did nothing at first. As it continued—got worse in fact—she excused herself from her recumbent patient and went to see what was going on.

In the waiting-room she stood and stared, amazed at the sight that met her eyes. The big box of toys had been upset in the middle of the floor. Magazines, most of them torn, were scattered on top, while round the walls, using the seats of the chairs as stepping-stones, ran a boy of about four, emitting bang-bang shooting sounds. A young woman with streaked hair was trying to catch him.

Meg had come out from behind her counter and Sue was standing at the door of the treatment room. Two patients, still waiting to be seen, were looking alarmed and cross in turn. 'Wants his arse tanned!' one of them shouted. The other, a frail old lady with sticks, levered them up and down.

Feeling her own temper rise, Kate made a grab for the boy. She caught him from behind and wrapped her arms round him, but reckoned without his flailing legs and hard heels, hammering at her shins, and had to let go of him. Meg lunged and grabbed at his coat, but he slipped out of it and into the passage, turning towards Guy's door.

'Oh, no... Quick... Sue, cut him off!' Kate heard herself shout, then three sounds seemed to come all at once—the opening of the door, Guy's loud exclamation and the frightened yelp of the child. He was borne out under Guy's arm, his struggles ignored. Into the waiting-room they came, across the strewn floor to the door.

'Whose child is this?' Guy's voice was soft, but still had a cutting edge.

'Darren's mine!' the young woman tried to take him.

'Then please follow me.' Out into the brisk windy morning they went. Guy set the child down in the drive, holding his arm till the mother had secured him. Meg came out with his coat. He was quiet now, but still looked mutinous and about to erupt again, swinging for his mother's hand and trying to lie on the ground.

'Take him home, please.' Guy began to retrace his steps to the door. 'Bring him this evening when he's calmed down or if you are the patient leave him at home. An uproar in my surgery can't be tolerated.'

All this Kate heard as she made her way back to her waiting patient, a forty-year-old woman with recurrent digestive problems. 'Sorry about that, Mrs Archer—case of a rampant child.'

'Sounded bad-tempered to me.'

Kate nodded and resumed palpating the woman's upper abdomen. 'Take a deep breath for me, please... Try and draw your ribcage up... That's right, good, that's fine. Any tenderness when I press here?'

'A little, yes... Not much, but yes. Is it an ulcer, do you think?'

'I don't know what it is, Mrs Archer. It's all right, you can get dressed now. What I think we'll do is refer you for a barium swallow.'

'At the hospital, you mean?'

'Yes, I'll get a letter off today. When you hear from the hospital they'll tell you not to eat for six hours before the appointment. The barium meal, as it's called, is a milky-looking liquid, usually flavoured to make it taste pleasant. While it's going through your digestive system a number of X-rays will be taken. Once your stomach is empty once more you'll be allowed to eat.'

'I see.' Lois Archer began to get dressed. 'So there's nothing that I need to do myself?' she said, looking round the screen at Kate.

'No, nothing,' Kate assured her. 'The date of the appointment will be sent to you direct from the hospital. All you have to do is wait, which is sometimes the hardest part.'

'It is for me, I'm the impatient sort!' Forcing a smile and trying to look cheerful, she thanked Kate and went out.

She was the last patient and Kate was checking her bag, before going out on her calls, when Sue put her head round the door and commented on the effective way Guy had dealt with the disruptive child. 'It was the Potts kid. Dr John has had trouble with him before. His mother doesn't seem to have a clue.'

'Oh, dear.' Kate added a nebuliser to her bag and snapped the clasps shut.

'Well, didn't you think Dr Guy was brilliant?' Sue went on.

'I suppose so,' Kate began, then stopped as a step in the passage heralded the arrival of Guy himself, whereupon Sue scuttled away.

'Didn't you approve of my hands-on method?' If anything, Guy sounded amused, which caused a little spurt of wrath in Kate.

She retorted, 'Well, to be truthful, Guy...' carefully

she slid her bag off the top of the desk '…I felt it was drastic, putting them both outside.'

'What would you have done, then?' His question was swift, catching her off guard.

'I'm not— I don't know, but—'

'Exactly,' he snapped. 'You didn't know! That racket had been going on for minutes before I came out!'

'Meg and I did our best, and so did the mother!' She made herself meet his eyes—hard, blue, glittery eyes.

'Not a very effective best.'

'You frightened him!' she accused hotly.

'Nonsense!' He turned on his heel.

'Shock tactics should never be resorted to with a child!'

'That little boy…' he swung round again '…was like an untrained pup. I doubt if he's ever been said no to in the whole of his short life!'

'It's pretty obvious you don't like children!'

'Now, look, Kate, let's have an end to this, shall we?' He moved forward to the desk, just as Sylvia tip-tapped into the room on high heels and in high spirits, oblivious to the atmosphere. She wasn't sensitive to very much.

'I heard a terrible shindig going on down here a few minutes ago.' Cream-suited and long-legged, she perched on the end of Kate's desk, looking elegant and sleek and years younger than her years. 'I thought you'd been set on by thugs.'

'One thug in the shape of a spoiled little boy.' Guy avoided Kate's eye.

'Kids these days!' Sylvia gave a theatrical flip with her hands. 'But that wasn't the reason I've come through, darling.' Now her gaze was all for Guy. 'I've had an idea, a good one, about you going to your father's wedding. Why not invite Kate to go along with you?

She's family, and she'd fit. Marcus told you to bring someone, didn't he? And she's the perfect choice.'

'Sylvia...' The name shot out of Kate in a strangled gasp. 'Sylvia, I've never met Mr Shearer. I couldn't possibly go!' She tried to say more, but somehow or other nothing else would emerge. As for Guy, he scarcely seemed to be listening.

'Think it over, that's all I ask.' Sylvia slipped down from the desk. '*Persuade* her, Guy. It's the right thing to do. Families should unite.'

'You've chosen a bad moment, Ma.' Guy slipped an arm about her shoulders and eased her to the door. 'We'll talk about it later.' He didn't glance around as he spoke, but went out after his mother. Kate heard him start up the car.

What a clot Sylvia was, Kate fumed as she headed towards the housing estate where she had two calls to make before lunch. What's she trying to do—couple Guy and me? Neither of us wants that. It's not that I dislike him—memories of yesterday's lunch swam into her mind—it's more that we don't, or aren't likely to, agree on important issues. If we were together much we'd quarrel. It's far better to keep our distance and remain on an even keel. As for this morning's fracas with the Potts child, perhaps he'd had right on his side.

Over lunch at home at Riverstone Lodge she told her mother about Sylvia's gaffe. 'Guy was furious with her, I could tell by his face.'

'Well, actually...' Laura spooned caramel custard onto Kate's plate '...I think it's a good idea. It's a Saturday so there's no problem about the surgery. It would be interesting to meet Guy's father. You'd probably both have a rattling good time. It wouldn't be much fun for Guy, going on his own.'

'He may have someone else in mind...to take, I mean.' Kate dabbed at a blob of custard on her white blouse.

'Well, he might, yes, and in that case he'll say so *and* tell his mother off—in private, of course.' Laura looked reflective. 'I must admit she does tend to put her foot in it sometimes, high heels and all.'

Kate laughed, aware that her mother and Sylvia, although the best of friends, were as diverse in nature as it was possible to be. When two friends weren't on the same wavelength closeness was hard to achieve.

She had her asthma clinic that afternoon, which took her up to four o'clock. It was her turn for evening surgery, too, and, after swallowing a cup of tea, she had a word with Miss Ford, the elderly evening receptionist, who told her who was coming.

'I had to squeeze Claire Potts in as an extra,' she apologised. 'She rang just now, asking for an appointment tonight. She's got trouble with her ear. I told her you were fully booked, but when she said she was in pain and felt generally unwell I felt I had to give in.'

'Quite right.' Kate nodded.

'She's a *Miss* Potts, Doctor—a single mum with a little boy. Lives with her parents in Swan Lane.'

'She was here this morning to see Dr Shearer, but left without being seen. The child was...restive.' Kate left it at that, but Miss Ford knew all about Darren as Sue had filled her in.

'She'll probably leave him at home tonight. Her parents will be back from work. They're decent people, but the child's been spoiled rotten from birth.' Which confirmed Guy's diagnosis *and* treatment. Was the man *ever* wrong? Kate wondered, sighing a little and feeling uncharitable.

Promptly at four-thirty she pressed her buzzer for the

first patient, and by the time Claire Potts came in she had seen no fewer than six—four with chest complaints, a pregnant woman in her thirty-eighth week, a care assistant with low back pain and a girl with dysmenorrhoea. 'Sit down, Miss Potts. What seems to be the trouble?' Kate smiled encouragingly, noting the girl's flushed face and general febrile appearance.

'I've got earache—had it for a few days. Keeps me awake at night, makes popping sounds too.' She spoke stiffly, as though nervous of relaxing her face.

'Any discharge…anything coming out of it?' Kate reached for her auriscope.

'No…haven't noticed any.' She looked alarmed as Kate came to stand by her chair.

'It's all right, Miss Potts, I just want to look down it with this little light. I shan't go anywhere near the painful area. Just hold very still and keep your head upright. Good, that's exactly right.'

Claire had cloudy dark hair which Kate moved aside, positioning the auriscope to obtain a clear view of the eardrum, which looked much as she'd expected—inflamed with a network of swollen blood vessels. Small wonder the girl was in pain.

'You've got a nasty infection…' she flicked off the auriscope light '…but it's at an early stage so we can stop it spreading with an antibiotic. I'll also give you something for the pain.'

'What is it exactly? Can Darren catch it?' Claire asked quickly.

'It's called otitis media and, no, he can't. It's not contagious. It sometimes comes after a cold or flu.'

'Yes, that's what I've had—a cold, I mean.'

'Well, there you are, then!' Kate smiled at her and handed over the prescription. 'Now, take the whole course of antibiotic, and if you're worried, or the trouble doesn't clear, come and see me again.'

'I usually see Dr John Burnett.'

'Yes, I know you're on his list, but he's off sick at the moment. Dr Shearer is taking his place.'

'The one who picked Darren up like a parcel?' An accusing eye met Kate's.

'Well, he *was* being rather noisy and boisterous.' Kate tried the effect of a smile.

'He was bored. He doesn't like waiting. I'd made a proper appointment and we didn't reckon on waiting. Anyway, he wasn't that bad. There was no need to put him outside.'

Not wanting to prolong the conversation, Kate kept silent as her patient, with her face averted, tied a scarf over her ears. She managed to mutter ''goodnight'' and ''thanks'' on her way to the door, but her black leather back made a passable job of conveying more loudly than words what she felt about classy doctors who dared to find fault with her child.

Kate sighed, then forgot her as she stiffened herself to see her next and last patient of the evening—a woman of thirty-five, whose curettage results from the minor surgical procedure undertaken the week before had been found to be malignant, making hysterectomy imperative. Mentally she rehearsed her words, wishing the task wasn't hers. Even now, after nearly four years in practice, she had never got used to telling patients bad news... It was a horrid part of the job.

This evening, however, it was made easier by the patient herself—a stalwart little Scottish lady with freckles and a fringe. 'It's no more than I expected,' she said, barely letting Kate finish. 'I'll have whatever treatment is going. My old grandma lived to ninety-five, and I can tell you this—I mean to do the same, Doctor. I'm no for dying yet.' She went out determinedly, if not cheerfully, to rejoin her husband in the waiting-room—a little red-haired, stalwart man, looking exactly like herself. They went off down the rainswept drive swaddled in mackintoshes, walking close and holding hands.

Watching them from the window, Kate dwelt on the fact that any news, be it glad or sad, was the better for sharing, for having someone to turn to. In the case of bad news, warm arms and a voice in one's ear, speaking comforting words, made all the difference.

With their duties concluded, the staff went off home. Shortly afterwards, with the rain sloshing down on her bare head, Kate was locking the outside door when a car drew up. Turning, she saw Guy at the wheel of the Rover, its nose turned towards the gates. I expect he's going out to supper, she thought as he opened the near-side door, letting it swing wide. 'Get in, Kate. I'd like a word. Look sharp, you're getting wet!'

Why get in? What for? she thought as she climbed into the car. Are we going to resume our fight about the Potts kid or…even worse…is he going to mention his father's wedding? Oh, please, not that!

She was wet about the top regions, droplets of rain trickling from her fringe to her brows and lashes. She tried to blow them away. 'I'm soaking the seat.'

'Think nothing of it!' Guy's words were the jesting kind, but he didn't smile or look at her and she couldn't get his measure. As for the rain, it had increased to a roar and hit the car as though it hated the sight of it, shrouding the windows in mist.

'What did you have in mind,' she asked flippantly, 'ferrying me along to my car?' She pushed her wet hair off her forehead, setting her medical case on the floor.

'In part, yes.' He let in the clutch and the car inched

forward. 'Why in heaven's name did you park it halfway down the drive?'

'When I came back from lunch my space had been invaded by a builders' lorry.' She glanced at him. He had stopped by her car so now she must get out—when she'd heard what he wanted, that was…

'You're not off to see a patient, are you?' she asked by way of a prompt. 'I'm the one on call, remember, up until Sunday night?'

'I remember, and I'm not.' He swung round to face her. 'I'm off to Town to see Pa, staying there overnight.'

'Oh, sorry, I wasn't being nosy,' she apologised, abashed.

'He'll want to know who I'm bringing with me—to the wedding, I mean.' Guy looked enquiringly at her, his dark brows dead level, the eyes beneath them as blue as the sky on a midsummer morning…eyes to drown in, compelling eyes. Kate felt faint…

'Sylvia shouldn't have said what she did,' she choked. 'Please don't feel—'

'Leave Ma out of it,' he interrupted, his bulky shoulders rasping against the back of his seat as he turned frontwards again. 'It's to be a register office affair, with a buffet lunch afterwards. There'll be interesting folk there on both sides. I'd…I'd like to have you with me. You might even…' he touched her wrist lightly '…find it enjoyable. If you don't, well, it'll all be done and dusted by mid-afternoon so there'll be plenty of time to get back here for anything else you've got planned.'

Kate felt warm all over, inside as well, like a kind of glow. Guy wanted her with him, which made her want to go. He could be great company…*was* great company. She recalled yesterday's lunch. Her toes curled in her shoes, and she knew that no way was she going to turn him down.

'And as to not knowing my father...' Guy smote the wheel with the heel of his hand. 'He'll love to meet you and so will other members of my family. I've met most of yours, remember. It'll be a chance to even the score. Still, of course, if you don't want to come...' Kate panicked a little then.

'I'd like to come very much indeed,' she said so emphatically that astonishment sat plain on his face as he turned to face her again.

'There now, I was getting all ready for a slap-down.' He grinned. 'Why, you've even shocked the rain into stopping. See, it's turned itself off like a tap.'

'So it has,' Kate said flatly, feeling that way as well. He wouldn't have minded all that much if she *had* turned him down. Didn't he ever, she wondered, take anything seriously, apart from his work? 'I'd better get out. Thanks for the lift.' She flung the words at him over her shoulder.

'A mere matter of yards, hardly a lift.' Her rain-darkened hair was parting in even swathes as she bent to pick up her bag. She was opening the door with painstaking care so as not to graze her own car, and was about to step out when she heard him ask, 'Was it an optical illusion on my part or did I see our harassed Mrs Potts leaving around half past five?'

'*Miss* Potts and, yes, you saw her.' Kate was holding the door ajar. 'She's got an ear infection and I prescribed penicillin. She'd left the boy at home.'

'I'm glad she came back,' Guy merely said, waiting until Kate was clear of the car and getting into her own, before driving off with a brief salute. His enquiry about Claire Potts led Kate to wonder if he'd had one or two misgivings about the little boy. Not that she had herself for, with the benefit of hindsight, she could see that he had been right. When people were ill, and waiting to be seen, and most likely worried as well, the last thing they wanted was a yelling small boy, driving them up the wall.

Over supper that evening she told her mother that she'd be going to the wedding after all. 'He brought it up again, did he?' Laura spooned parsley sauce over her fish.

'Yes, just now.'

'Good for him, I thought he would. I've been thinking, Kate, we ought to have them over for a meal—John, Sylvia and Guy.'

'Should we?' Kate stopped chewing.

'I thought Sunday week for lunch. I could get a leg of lamb and stuff it, and make some of that *crème brûlée* your uncle likes so much.'

'Sounds as if you've got it all worked out.'

'I have, and I want to do it. If your father were here he'd be all for it—he loved family gatherings. Also, of course, we ought to make the most of Guy while he's here. Once he's finished the locum he'll probably go shooting off abroad again.'

'Yes, perhaps he will.' Kate waited for relief to wash over her at this point, and it did, but dismay was strong within it and she was forced to realise that, despite Guy's quirks and undoubted bossiness, she would miss him when he went.

CHAPTER FOUR

As THINGS turned out, the Larchwood contingent, as Laura dubbed them, were already booked for Sunday week so the family get-together was fixed for the evening of 5 November, becoming supper instead of lunch.

'I feel,' Laura said, when Kate came in after evening surgery, 'that I ought to be serving up jacket spuds by a bonfire in the orchard.' It was the fifth of November, and already, at only seven p.m., most firework parties were under way. Kate had driven home under the thrusting whine of rockets, tearing into the sky.

'Somehow I can't see Sylvia entering into the spirit of fireworks.' Kate hurried upstairs to change into her black velvet palazzo pants and shiny satin shirt. Her hair swung and gleamed as she brushed it, her skin looked like pink pearl above the dark of her outfit and she made up her eyes with care.

She was fixing her earrings when she heard the car and Merle's whining bark, then the front door opening and her mother's voice, greeting their guests. They had come...they were here...*he* was here! With a feeling of butterflies inside, she moved across the room and made for the stairs.

Down in the hall her mother was taking Sylvia's fur jacket. Her uncle, released at last from the confines of his neck collar, was looking up the stairs for her, his plastered arm showing up white. As for Guy, he was bending down to Merle who was allowing herself to be petted. Since the spirited Sparky had been rehomed, Merle had come into her own.

'We've decided to keep her,' Kate said, joining the little group. 'No one wanted to give a home to so ancient a dog.'

'Except us, and we love her, tunnel vision and all.' Laura came out of the cloakroom, still in her butcher blue apron and made for the kitchen door.

'I really admire the way you do all that voluntary work,' Sylvia commented, following at her heels.

'Anyone can do it. There are loads of vacancies,' Laura pointed out without rancour or malice, making Sylvia laugh.

'I'm a drone and know it. I wasn't always, but John encourages sloth!'

'You have enough to do, looking after me. Anyway, you're gems, both of you.' John linked his good arm in his wife's, and asked Laura what was cooking. 'Something smells out of this world and my taste buds are going mad!'

'And how are you this evening?' Guy enquired of Kate as they stood in the window, watching the fireworks bursting in the garden next door.

'Pretty much the same as I was at the practice meeting earlier.'

'But people seem different in different settings,' he said, and she knew what he meant. It wasn't so much a matter of appearance as of manner, she decided. Guy, for instance, looked as he did usually—large, dark and well groomed—but his social demeanour was a whole world apart from his workaday GP one. On the job he was very much Dr Shearer. Here, in her home, against the comfortable background of Riverstone Lodge, he was simply and solely Guy.

Over dinner, eating lamb so tender that it could have

been eaten with a spoon, Laura let slip that Kate was
looking out for a property to buy. 'As an investment,
Kate?' Sylvia enquired, reaching for her wine.

'No, to live in.' Kate wished her mother had kept
silent about her plan. Not that it was a state secret, exactly, but she had only just started looking, and it might
be some time before she found anything suitable.

'And before one of you asks…' Laura gave John a
second helping of meat. 'Before one of you asks if I
mind, of *course* I don't. I could hardly expect Kate to
prop me up for all time.'

'What are you looking for, Kate?' Guy enquired. 'A
flat, I suppose.'

'I suppose that would be the most suitable thing,' Kate
began. She was cut off by Sylvia, who laid down her
fork to say, 'This house is far too big for you, Laura.
Why not slice a portion off as a flat for Kate—in other
words, convert. It's the smart thing to do these days.'

'I like Riverstone as it is. I don't want to cut it up. I
don't want it spoiled,' Laura said with heightened colour, but Sylvia went on, undeterred.

'It needn't be spoiled. It could be done so skilfully
that it wouldn't look a scrap different, at least not from
the outside. I know a firm in Town who—'

'No, Sylvia, no *way*!' Laura looked ready to burst.

'Mummy doesn't want that, and neither do I,' Kate
interposed. 'She was happy with Dad here in the house,
exactly as it is! She doesn't want to change it, and alter
the…the *feel* of it.'

'Which is understandable.' Guy flashed a look at his
mother.

'Besides, I need the space for homing my four-legged
friends.' Laura was on an even keel again, grinning
cheerfully at Sylvia who, unwilling to give in, told her
the whole concept was ludicrous.

'Turning the place into a gigantic doghouse!'

'I think, my love, that Laura knows what she wants,' John said quickly, before Guy could explode. 'Now, Laura, sweetheart...' his big hand closed over hers on the damask cloth '...what are you going to give your brother-in-law for pud?'

So the little lively wind blew over, at least well enough, although it seemed to Kate, half an hour later when they were through in the sitting-room, that a whiff of it followed them in there as they made conversation over the coffee and mints and tiny macaroons.

When the phone rang in the hall Kate leapt up to answer it. She was on call, and it might be a patient. She rather hoped it was, and her hope, or wish, was granted for, after listening carefully to the voice on the other end of the line, she reached for her coat and bag. Putting her head round the sitting-room door, she announced that she was off. 'Emergency call...a burned child and a grandfather in collapse!'

'Two patients at the same address?' Guy was on his feet.

'Yes, it was a firework party.'

'Then I'll come with you,' he announced. 'You may need help. You can't attend to two patients at once.'

Kate didn't argue. It was obvious that Guy wanted out as much as she did. 'I can do with some fresh air,' he commented, settling himself in her car.

'More acrid than fresh tonight, alas,' Kate shouted above the scream of a rocket, tearing into the sky.

'A baptism of fire.' He fastened his belt as they started off down the drive. 'Who are the patients—do I know them?'

'The old man, Mr Stanhope, is on Uncle's list. He's on treatment for hypertension. The little girl, Nell, and her mother usually see me.'

'In that case, I'll take Mr Stanhope and you the girl.'

Once again Kate didn't argue, even though the call was hers. What did it matter so long as both patients were treated speedily?

'You'll have to share my bag,' she said, taking the roundabout at reckless speed and making Guy gasp.

'Want me to drive?' he asked.

'I think I can manage *that* without assistance. Besides, you've been drinking,' she reminded him with a certain relish.

'I've had one drink,' he corrected, laughing, but said no more till they drew up at a redbrick end-of-terrace house that Kate remembered visiting in the summer when the child, Nell, had been recovering from a tonsillectomy.

This evening there were lights both upstairs and down. In the long front garden a bonfire smouldered, and as they walked up the path Nell's mother, Mrs Stanhope, flung open the door, hardly giving Kate time to introduce Guy before telling them what had happened. 'Nell fell and caught her hand on a hot firework. My father-in-law was with her and he just…seemed to collapse. My husband and brother carried him in—he's through in the back. Nell's upstairs with a schoolfriend. She's been sick and is very upset.'

The small house was full of people, most of them in the room to the right of the passage. They stared out at Kate and Guy. There were others moving about in the kitchen at the end and there was a smell that could have been burgers or sausages. There was very little in the way of talking and no laughter at all.

Guy went through to see Mr Stanhope, while Kate was taken upstairs by his daughter-in-law, Ann Stanhope, to see the little girl, who was sitting on the side of her bed, still in her anorak. Another child, sitting beside her, jumped up when they approached and ran downstairs at a gallop, as though glad to be out of the way. Ann who by now had calmed down, removed a bowl from her daughter's lap.

'You remember Dr Kate, don't you, love?'

'Sort of.' The child looked at Kate, her hair lying flat and limp on either side of her tear-streaked face. 'I've burnt my hand. It hurts!' She was guarding it, making a wall with her other hand.

'I know you have, and burns are painful, especially when they've only just happened.' Kate sat beside her, trying to gain her confidence. 'Could you lay your hand on my lap, do you think, so I can see what the damage is?'

Nell complied reluctantly, giving every appearance of wanting to snatch it back again, but a swift glance at the reddened skin gave Kate her answer at once. Nell had suffered a second-degree burn, mainly of the palm of her hand but also involving three of her fingers and the base of her thumb.

'Well, you're going to have blisters, Nell, and that's for real,' she said lightly but sympathetically, not wanting to frighten the child. 'I'm afraid it means a trip to Casualty.' She looked over at Ann. 'They'll have all the right dressings for it, and they'll give Nell something for shock.'

'Can my husband and I drive her there?' Ann looked distressed.

'Of course,' Kate replied, just as Don Stanhope burst into the room, looking across at his wife.

'It's as we thought, Ann.' He sounded breathless. 'Dad's had a stroke. The doctor's got him a bed in the General and has rung for an ambulance. Can you pack him a bag? I'll get back to him.' He made to go out of the room, then spotted his daughter and retraced his steps. 'And what about you, Mouse?' He stroked her hair.

'She's got to go to Casualty. I'll take her—I expect you'll be going with Dad.' Ann was looking flurried again. Nell wanted to know if her grandfather was going to die.

'Absolutely not,' her father answered quickly. 'In no time at all you'll both be out dangling rods over that riverbank again. They're angling buddies,' he said to Kate as Guy entered the room.

'The ambulance is here, Mr Stanhope. They're getting your father out.' He smiled at Nell as she slipped off the bed, sympathising with her about her hand, saying, as Kate had done, that burns were painful wounds.

Within five minutes the last of the guests had left the house and the ambulance had drawn away with the Stanhopes' car in its wake. Only Kate and Guy were left at the gate, and presently they drove off under a sky still under attack, smoke seeping into the car.

'This business of gunpowder, treason and plot has reached daft proportions,' Guy growled, as Kate took the bridge at a snail's pace because of a crowd of small boys who were brandishing fireworks like medieval flares and throwing them at the car.

'I used to enjoy it,' Kate said stoutly, then changed the subject, by asking what he'd thought of the elderly Mr Stanhope.

'Not too good.' Guy eased himself more comfortably in his seat. 'The bleed has affected his dominant side so, as a righthanded person, he'll be very incapacitated with a useless right arm and leg. His speech centre is affected and he plainly has no awareness of his surroundings. At a guess I would say the prognosis is poor, and he may slip into a coma.'

'How terrible. He's not that old.'

'Sixty-six. Doubtless, seeing his granddaughter hurt precipitated the stroke. The son said he and the girl were close and spent a lot of time together. That kind of closeness sometimes comes with a skipped generation.'

'Uncle John knows the family well. He'll be very sorry about it.'

There was a short silence, then Guy asked, 'Are we making for home?'

'Why, yes, where else?' Kate glanced at him. What was in his mind?

'Let's make a slight detour. Turn down Fallerton Road—there's a house there up for sale. I know about it from the owner, a patient of John's. He and his wife are emigrating to New Zealand next month.'

'Why the interest?' Kate asked, but she slowed to make the turn.

'I thought *you* might be interested, bearing in mind what you said earlier on about getting your own place.'

'Not a house.' Kate was startled and showed it. 'And not nearly so soon. I was thinking more in terms of a flat or a small…or something small.'

'In that case, a house wouldn't do, but we can still drive past it, slow down and take a look. The owners are away. They're living in London till they fly out next month.'

'You're not acting as their agent, are you?' Kate asked, trying to laugh.

'No, it's in Perry & Company's hands. If I'm anyone's agent I'm yours.'

'Thanks!'

'Don't mention it!'

The light-hearted words flipped back and forth between them. Kate was thinking, I couldn't possibly afford to buy a house. Not yet, it's too soon. On the other hand, Fullerton Road, along which they were now driv-

ing, was roughly midway between Melbridge and
Grantford, perfectly placed for the surgery *and* for keeping an eye on her mother. It might be worth taking a
look.

The house, called Mayfield, was on a corner plot, and
they could see it quite plainly by the light of a nearby
streetlamp. It looked attractive and solidly robust with
its white walls and green pantile roof. A satellite dish
stuck out at one end, and there was a conservatory on
the side. The front garden of lawns and flower-beds
looked neat and compact.

It's a great house and I could manage the garden. The
thought swam teasingly into Kate's mind. Out loud she
said, 'They'll probably want the earth for a place like
that.'

'They don't. They want a quick sale.' Guy was un-
doing his belt. 'Let's have a look round the back, shall
we? There's plenty of light.'

Kate hung back. 'It's trespassing.'

'But in their interests, surely. Oh, come on, Kate, stir
yourself. We won't get arrested tonight—the police are
far too busy, answering emergency calls.'

As they walked up the front path and round to the
back, so fanciful had Kate's mood become that she could
have sworn the little house huffed a welcome, twinkled
its windows and juddered its roof. The back garden was
as tidy as the front, and there were two trees which could
have been may. They would cream with blossom in the
spring, Kate thought as she touched the bark of one.
'Turn yourself around and look at the house, not the
garden,' Guy said. She did so, standing in front of him
and feeling his hands light upon her shoulders. Yes...
yes, it was a perfect house.

'It's too big for one.' She sounded defensive.

'You can't tell till you've seen the inside. Anyway, in the course of time you may join up with someone again.'

'If you mean what I think you mean, I won't—at least, not for years and years.' She moved away from him and his hands left her shoulders, but she felt him close behind.

'What really went wrong between you and Mike?' Guy asked, and Kate felt herself freeze, so much so that she stopped walking to try and rustle up offputting words.

'I told you, he went to America and as I didn't want to practise medicine over there we agreed to kiss and part!' She hoped she sounded flippant and uncaring. Probably she did for his following comment was distinctly pro-Mike.

'If you'd thought enough of the poor chap you'd have gone with him.'

'You know nothing about it!' she flashed, and for a second she was tempted to tell him the truth, if only to prove him wrong. Instead she whipped enough anger to hit back at him, even to scoff as she did so. 'What about you?' she asked. 'You're not going to tell me that there wasn't some fascinating female in Mtanga who wanted you to stay on.'

'I'm not because there was,' he said clearly, looking up into the sky as he followed the ascent of a rocket before its colourful burst.

His jaw was rigid, and she should have shut up, but some devil forced her to say, 'Then the same applies to you, doesn't it? If you'd loved her enough you'd have stayed.'

'I'd never let any woman get in the way of my work prospects and decisions.'

'So, that comes first?'

'It does.'

'And the woman has to tag along like a tail?' She made to walk on, but he seized her and turned her, closing the space between them.

'You're oversimplifying!'

'I'm not!'

'Shut up!' His words slurred against her ear till he took her chin between finger and thumb and covered her mouth with his.

She struggled at first, then ceased to do so. Pliant in his arms, she rested against his long, hard body, feeling its fit on hers, the joy it infused and the urgency, but not for very long. With a swift, almost violent movement she wrested herself from his hold.

'I loathe being kissed in anger!' She backed against the hedge, feeling the scrape of its twigs on her anorak and her heels sinking into the earth.

'Then you shouldn't provoke it. I'm human—as plainly you are.' His voice was low and quite undisturbed, which fired her again.

'I don't know what you mean. I don't even like you. I never *have* liked you!'

'Who's talking about liking?' He came close again, 'Oh, come on, Kate, grow up and give me your keys. I'm driving us home whether you like it or not!'

She never knew why she succumbed at that. She dropped the keys into his palm in case she touched him, and walked past him to the gate.

On the short drive home he spoke of the patients they'd seen, which both relieved and frustrated Kate in just about equal proportions. Surely he couldn't ignore what had happened. Surely he could feel the tension between them which made her head sing as though someone had boxed her ears.

'How about calling a truce?' he suggested as they drew up outside Riverstone. 'We need to get on, don't we, for the sake of our patients? I mean, we don't want them collapsing from uncomfortable vibes in the passage between our two rooms.'

'That would never do.' She managed to laugh and take the hand he held out, which had been meant to shake hers but which withdrew itself before she could get a good grip.

'Fireworks have a lot to answer for,' he muttered, clambering out of the car.

Nothing, Kate vowed to herself that night, will induce me to buy that house. If it was offered to me at a give-away price, my answer would be the same. So it was surprising that next day, in the single hour she was able to glean between her home visits and evening surgery, she contacted the estate agent, told him she was interested and would like to view it at once.

She took her mother with her, not so much for her advice but to make her feel part of it all and in no way shut out. Mr Perry, in the manner of all estate agents, extolled its many virtues as he guided them from sitting-room to dining-room, to kitchen and up to the three bed-rooms. Long before he had finished, Kate knew she wanted it, not just a little but passionately. She had fallen in love with it.

Laura agreed it was a little gem. Even so, she voiced some doubts. 'A whole house, Kate, on your own. You'll be lost in it,' she said.

'Plenty of women on their own live in "whole houses", Mummy, and the price is right—in fact, amazingly low,' Kate whispered as they went back downstairs.

'I'll be inundated with applicants once the advert comes out tomorrow,' Mr Perry, who had long ears, called up from the hall. 'Mr and Mrs Rolfe want a quick sale so it'll be first come first served.'

'Subject to contract and survey, I'll take it. I'm offering the full asking price.' Kate's voice practically rang out, further alarming Laura who felt she should have thought about it for a day or two more.

'I know I want it and to delay might be fatal.' Kate whisked past Mr Perry, stepping out into the dusk of the garden as though it were hers already. There, near the gate, where the hedge was bashed, Guy had seized and kissed her... And she had kissed him and had wanted more... Of course, he had known it. Sometimes she felt he knew everything about her, and she hated that most of all.

'You look flushed, darling. Don't get too excited in case things don't work out. Buying a house is dicey,' Laura warned. 'So many things can go wrong.'

'Yes, I'll bear that in mind!' The first of the street-lamps flickered on as the three of them parted at the gate—Kate to the surgery, Laura home to Riverstone and Mr Ernest Perry back to his office in the high street to telephone the Rolfes.

Kate's surgery that evening was uneventful, most of the patients presenting with seasonal ailments—coughs and colds and flu. One man only gave cause for special concern. He was a smoker. 'Been smoking for years, I'm a forty-a-day man,' he announced with a certain pride. 'Can't at the moment, though, all I do is choke. This last day or two I've been spitting blood, and the wife don't think that's right.'

'It certainly is *not* right.' Kate reached for her stethoscope. 'Will you take off your coat and shirt for me, please, then lean your arms on the desk and bend right over them so I can sound your chest from the back.'

He did so, and she asked him to breathe in with his mouth open. 'Good, now out...now in...now out... Just once more, please!' She ran her fingers over the rib area, then went back to her chair.

'Is it bronchitis, then?' For the first time Mr Higham looked anxious.

'Possibly.' Kate's eyes were downcast as she wrote out a prescription. 'This is for an antibiotic, which will help clear the infection, but you also need an X-ray. The hospital will send you an appointment. It's best to know what we're treating.' She looked up and smiled, handing him the prescription and trying to mask her concern for she knew that his symptoms might indicate the presence of a growth on his lung.

The last patient was a middle-aged woman, recovering from shingles, who needed sympathy and reassurance more than anything else, plus a repeat prescription for her DF118 painkiller and tablets rich in vitamin B.

Miss Ford, the evening receptionist, went home, and Kate was preparing to leave herself when Guy came through from the house to tell her that Mr Stanhope had died. 'I called at the hospital to see him, but was told he'd had a massive stroke shortly after four o'clock.'

'Oh, dear, I'm sorry, but it was as you thought. I mean, you didn't think much of his chances, did you?' Kate was thinking of the little girl, Nell, as she looked across at Guy.

'I didn't, no.' He took her coat from her and held it out for her to slip on. 'You'll need this. The temperature's dropping—it'll most likely freeze tonight.'

'Yes, well, it's winter.' Kate shivered, but not with cold. His fingers had grazed her neck, and she was battling against the sensations his touch had aroused...little pinpricks of pleasure and pain. Her back was turned to him as she fastened her coat and turned up the collar, but he was close behind her and she could feel him there. She jumped when he spoke again.

'And how are *you* this evening, Kate?'

She turned round and said she was fine. 'Why do you ask?' Her eyes challenged his.

'No reason, just checking.' He smiled.

It was an affable, innocuous kind of smile, and it made her feel easier. In no time at all she found herself telling him about the house. 'I've decided to have it...paying the asking price. I'm seeing about the mortgage tomorrow. Mr Perry says if there are no hold-ups over searches I may get possession in a month.'

'Before Christmas, then.' Guy gave a half-whistle.

'Fingers crossed, yes, although I don't suppose I'll move in till New Year. I may want to decorate.' Kate went on jerkily, nervous under his gaze.

'Of course, yes, there are always things that need to be done.' Guy began to move to the door that led through to the house. Not wanting him to disappear, at least not quite so soon, Kate called his name, making him turn to face her again.

'It's just that I wanted to say thanks for telling me about the house. I mean, I wouldn't have known...and I really am grateful to have been told about it so soon.'

'That's what friends...sorry, correction...that's what *colleagues* are for, but if it makes you feel any less indebted to me, Kate, it was the Rolfes' interests I served.'

'Well, yes, of course, I know,' Kate swallowed, feeling the cold wash of rebuff.

'Now, about Saturday,' he went on, jerking his sweater cuff free of his watch. 'I suggest we go up to Town by train, using taxis each end. It'll solve the parking problem and the drinking one as well. I don't want to have to refuse to drink on my father's wedding day.'

'No. I mean, yes, I agree.' Kate smiled as he wished her goodnight and made his way down the passage and through the house door at the end. He was wishing he hadn't asked her to the wedding—his whole manner told her that. She'd been rude to him the night before...not that he hadn't deserved it. Even so, she wasn't green, and she could have handled the situation better. That handshake of theirs had patched things up, but the truce was a fragile one.

CHAPTER FIVE

WEDDINGS and funerals were emotional occasions and had a habit of breaking down barriers so perhaps that was why, after Marcus Shearer and his bride had been waved off by their guests, Guy suggested to Kate that they spent a few hours in London, enjoying themselves. 'It seems a shame to waste all this party mood and just go home.'

'I couldn't agree more.' Kate thrilled to his words and smiled up at him. What an amazing day this had turned out to be! Right from the very start, when Guy had called for her in the taxi which had whisked them to the station, everything had been perfect. *He* had been perfect. There had been no awkwardness, no two-edged remarks, just lovely compliments and male attentiveness, which had naturally made her feel good.

Kate was wearing a soft-as-velvet suede suit in rich chocolate brown—a perfect foil for her gold hair and clear, pale skin. 'I'll be the envy of every male in sight,' Guy had told her, wrenching his gaze from her long legs in lustre tights so unnervingly close to his own.

She had certainly turned heads at the wedding. Marcus had been enchanted. 'She's a peach of a girl, Guy, my boy, but looks no more like a country GP than you do, come to that.'

'GPs come in all shapes and sizes, Pa, and Kate is a very good one,' Guy said, watching her wend her way back to them after talking to a distinguished author with a pointed beard who wrote novels about the occult.

It was three-thirty and dusk was falling when they

finally left the windy heights of the Hampstead Hotel for the clamour of the West End. They visited the National Gallery first, spent an hour in a news theatre, then crossed the river to a restaurant at the top of one of the tower blocks.

It had been designed to resemble the inside of an ocean liner, with its louvred ceiling and sloping windows looking across the Thames to the heart of the City area. The great dome of St Paul's stood in full-bodied glory against the glow of the night sky. Far below, the river itself, dappled and streaked with lights, flowed with seemingly no movement at all under London Bridge.

'What a view!' Kate exclaimed, for they could see it to full advantage as they sat side by side at their banquette table, eating grilled crevettes. They were served with wafer-thin brown bread and butter and a light white wine, which Guy pointed out was the best thing to have after so much wedding champagne.

After nearly eight hours in Guy's company Kate was feeling more at ease with him. He had been...was being...flatteringly attentive. He knew how to treat a woman but, then, of course, he'd have had plenty of practice—a man like him.

She wondered about the girlfriend he'd left behind in Africa. Had he been very upset when she'd elected to stay over there? Did she write to him or he to her? Had the break been total? She suddenly wanted to know so much that she very nearly asked him, but was saved by him telling her that he'd been to The Summit restaurant before. 'Oh, have you?' She pricked up her ears, and swallowed some wine.

'With my father and Jean soon after I got back to England. We were eating at sunset then, which was spectacular.'

'I can imagine.'

'Although the night lends softness and mystery.' He turned his face to hers. Sitting so close she could see herself reflected in his eyes, see the little lines splaying out from their corners, the bendy ones round his mouth—a firm, yet sensual mouth with a slightly full bottom lip. I wish I wasn't so drawn to him. I wish I could be more in control, not blowing hot and cold just because he's near. 'Everything seems different at night,' she managed to say, keeping her voice level and her thoughts at bay while she added more warmly, 'And nothing could improve on this.'

'So, you're glad you came?' He refilled her glass.

'Absolutely!' she said.

'Even though,' he persisted gently, 'you don't like me very much?'

He was fishing, of course. 'I like you all right.' She didn't intend to give too much ground, at least not all at once, but she did go on to say, 'If you're referring to Tuesday, I was just being childish. I don't usually behave like that.'

He was saved from comment by the waiters, arriving to collect their empty plates—two very deft and dexterous waiters who flipped and flapped about and made a draught, then departed at speed. During the brief interval before they came back Guy pointed out various landmarks, including the Walbrook Hospital and the medical school, lying a little behind.

'Where you trained,' she said, not at all sure that she was looking at the right spot.

'My old stamping ground, yes.'

'I wasn't lucky enough to get into a London medical school, but I was very happy at Mamesbury. Wiltshire's a beautiful county, and the practice I joined was friendly.' Kate gabbled on doggedly as the waiters were returning with their main course of roast grouse and mixed vegetables.

During the rest of the meal Guy asked her about her earlier years, and so disarmed was she by his interest that once they'd got to the coffee stage she decided to come clean and tell him the truth about Mike. In a sense Guy himself paved the way by asking her if she had any regrets about leaving the Wiltshire firm.

'No, because if I'd stayed there,' she replied, 'I'd have seen Mike round every corner.'

'But I thought...' He looked puzzled. 'I thought you said—'

'Oh, I mean seen him inside my head. You see, it wasn't exactly as I told you. I didn't refuse to go to America with him. He went with someone else—a physiotherapist from Massachusetts who'd been working with him in hospital on a six months' exchange arrangement. Her name was Caroline Ellenburgh, and we had her to the flat once or twice.

'She was a typical American—friendly, easy to get on with. She wasn't especially attractive, though, and it never occurred to me, not for one single moment, that she was any kind of threat. Her father was an osteopath/physio in Boston with three private clinics, two of them in Maine. She told us about them, talked about them. I could tell Mike was interested, but I still wasn't prepared for what came out of it all. When she was due to go back she took him with her.

'There was a job lined up for him at the Boston clinic where she also worked so off he went, giving me only an hour's notice before leaving the flat. I felt...' Kate's voice trembled slightly. 'I felt as though I'd been shot.'

'Dear God!' Guy stiffened beside her.

'Sorry I lied.'

One of his hands pulled hers down onto his lap. 'The fellow must have been crazy!'

'You don't have to be gallant.'

'Gallantry doesn't come into it. I'm saying what I think. Are you still in love with him?' His grip on her hand was tight.

'I don't know,' she said simply. 'It all seems to have happened a very long time ago to a different person...to a different me. It's very difficult to explain.'

Guy made a growling sound in his throat and released Kate's hand. 'I hope his new job bored the pants off him,' he said, gulping down some water.

'I hoped that at first. I wanted everything to go wrong for him. I was as angry as I was hurt. I was surprised how vitriolic I could be, but I *am* sorry I lied—to you, I mean. It was a kind of defence.'

'You are entirely forgiven,' he said lightly, touching her hand again. 'As a matter of fact, my liaison in Africa wasn't exactly as I led you to suppose. I wanted Julie, the nursing sister in the unit, to come back with me. Admittedly we hadn't been together for as long as you and Mike, but we were close enough—or so I thought— and my pride took a knock when she told me she loved Africa and was signing on for another spell out there. She was entirely cool about it and, like you, I was hurt and furious.'

'Oh, dear!'

'Yes, exactly... Oh, dear!' he mocked, but his eyes were twinkling. Suddenly they were laughing together, and a great sense of ease seemed to enter Kate's mind and body, ousting hurt and rejection and building up her confidence to new heights. 'Has anyone special succeeded Mike?' he asked after a pause.

She shook her head. *He* was special—or could be— and she knew it. He could be special, but don't fall in love with him, her cautious inner voice warned. He'll be gone by the New Year, most likely abroad again... *Don't fall in love with him.*

In the taxi that bore them off to the station some fifteen minutes later, he threw out the suggestion that they ought to console one another. 'When we're both off at a weekend we could come up here perhaps, do a show, have supper, go to a club—anything you pleased. You've decided you no longer dislike me—' the old teasing note was back in his voice '—we have tastes in common and we're attracted to one another.'

Kate's heart began to jump. 'Are we?' she croaked.

'You know we are!'

She nodded. Of course she knew... Of course, of course, she knew. If I go out with him we'll end up in bed together. The thought passed through her mind in a series of swoops and she became dizzy. 'Perhaps we could talk about it later when we're more...ourselves,' she said.

'I'm myself now—never been more so. We'll discuss it on the train,' Guy said as their taxi got in line to move onto the station approach.

Their train was about to pull out when they reached their platform, and they had to get on at the rear. It was full, too, and they were unable to find two seats together. Guy was all for walking further up in the hope of better luck there, but Kate pointed out that it was highly unlikely there'd be more than standing room there. 'It's a stopping train so there'll be people getting out along the line,' she said, so they subsided in the available seats and made the best of it.

From her position across the aisle and a little back from Guy, Kate was able to look at him, unobserved, half closing her eyes. His head was turned away from her a little towards an elderly man by the window. He appeared to be listening intently, his strong, dark profile etched against the seat back. She saw him smile and her insides clutched. Even from this distance, even though the smile wasn't for her, she was moved by it, disturbed by it, and longed to be at his side.

The train trundled on. Most people were dozing, but Kate didn't so much as try. She had never felt more wide awake, despite their action-packed day. They must, she felt, be nearing Royle's Cross. Yes, she was right, they were. The train was braking, its wheels making a harsh cawing sound. One or two people were getting up, including the man next to Guy who was reaching for his overcoat, buttoning it as he stood. Doors were opening then banging shut and passengers were disembarking from other parts of the train. Kate could see them making for the exit and iron footbridge, some in evening dress. Guy was standing up and beckoning to her. She joined him at his seat, opposite an Indian girl in a sari and a middle-aged woman in black.

'That's better.'

'Much.' They smiled at one another. Guy linked his arm through Kate's, and they sat close, shoulder to shoulder. The Indian girl's finely boned face showed reflective interest, the sharp eyes of the middle-aged woman taking in Kate's suit.

Guy began to tell Kate that the man who'd sat next to him had been to a wedding too. 'Not one like Pa's and Jean's, but a full-scale white affair. The bride was his niece and he kept going on about all the expense involved.'

'A white wedding…romantic,' breathed Kate. In the absence of comment from Guy she went on to ask him where he thought his father and Jean were now. He looked at his watch, calculating the time difference.

'Most probably,' he said, 'at Lisbon Airport, waiting to be jetted to Madeira.'

'Lucky them, it should be warm there.'

'Around seventy at least so a good deal warmer than—' He got no farther than that for without warning—no warning at all—the train gave a massive jolt. There was a grinding and tearing, their carriage lurched sideways, branches of trees thrust through the windows, scattering glass, people screamed and the lights went out. Guy still held Kate fast, but they'd been flung to the floor. The Indian girl was half on top of them and Kate could feel the material of her sari lying over her face.

They were no longer moving. The spinning wheels were still. All round them passengers were struggling to their feet. There were terrified shouts and screams.

'We're off the rails!'

'We're leaning over!'

'We're going to tip!'

In a daze Kate felt Guy thrusting her towards one of the broken doorways. They were pushed and pummelled by people behind. The floor listed like a ship's deck, fallen luggage made stumbling blocks and their feet slipped and crunched on glass. Then came the drop down onto grass at the side of the track, before they were swept by the crowd through a thin belt of trees, emerging into a field which swelled and surged with people, frightened and distraught, while all along the train, as far as they could see, others fought to get out.

'What's happened?'

'What was it?'

'Have we hit another train?'

Cries rang out on all sides. Guy had tight hold of Kate's arm. The Indian girl and the woman who'd been sitting near her were standing just behind. It was impossible to see much at first, but as their eyes became used to the dark they could just make out other carriages, leaning like their own.

'It looks,' Guy said, straining to see the rest of the train, 'as though this, the back part, is uncoupled from the rest. As for the front, I can't see a thing. It's probably overturned!'

Kate's blood froze. 'Someone must have a phone…someone must have a mobile!' She and Guy shouted out above the babble of the crowd. Then other cries were heard from a group of people, running over from nearby houses. Help was on its way. Someone had phoned. The live current was off.

'Let's get further up and see what we can do.' Guy's voice came in jerks. Pushing through the trees to the trackside again, they walked up beside the train. It was rough going. The grass was lumpy and Kate's shoes were the flimsy kind. They were knocked and pushed into by other passengers, still jumping down from tilted carriages, but eventually they came to the break…to the space…to the severed section…to the front four carriages. Just for a second they halted and stared, all but deafened by cries for help, knocking and banging, the explosive breaking of glass.

The first coach was askew on top of the hulk of a fallen tree. The next three lay on their sides, windows uppermost like skylights, wheels still spinning at the sides. Passengers were escaping by smashing the windows, heaving themselves up and out and then crawling on hands and knees as they looked for ways to get down.

A girl with a child hanging round her neck screamed for someone to help her. Guy, stepping sideways over the rails, brought her back to Kate, who took the child through the trees to the field, trying desperately to see and stem the blood from a scalp wound. The mother was being sick. How to help, how best to help, how to help anyone, without lights, without equipment.

More and more injured were getting out, some falling out, all with tales of people trapped.

"Old chap with his chest stove in."

"Young girl stuck under a seat."

"An old woman too scared to shift."

'Help is coming, it's on its way,' Kate kept saying. She could just make out Guy a few feet away, bending over a shape on the ground. Then at last, dear God, at last, she heard the sirens. They were coming, they were coming, the ambulances were here. She could see their lights, see their white sides rocking at the road end of the field. They were followed by fire engines, police cars and vans. Hovering above the trees was a paramedic helicopter, preparing to land.

Powerful lights flooded the scene and the rescue teams sprang into action. The police with loudhailers dispersed the uninjured crowds. 'Follow the police vans along the side of the field to the road. There will be coaches laid on to take you to your destinations. Passengers with walking injuries please report to the ambulance team.'

Kate was never to forget the night of the Royle's Cross train disaster, but while it was all going on, while she and Guy were working alongside the rescue teams, there was no time for thought. It was all urgency, all action—like an A and E alert, yet more than that, worse than that, for they were right at the start of it all.

They were the ones to help sort out the dead from the injured, the seriously injured from the lesser kind, giving comfort when they could. They gave oxygen, injected drugs, immobilised broken limbs, fitted cervical collars, set up IV lines. They worked under ladders, pulleys and cranes; they worked amid the scream and whine of cutting equipment, the cries of victims in pain.

The ambulances journeyed backwards and forwards from two major hospitals. By three in the morning every passenger had been freed and taken off for treatment. Only the police and the firemen, and one or two helpers, like Kate and Guy, remained—and the train, of course, which Kate couldn't look at. 'What happened to everyone else, to the others in our section?' she asked, her voice grating with tiredness.

'Coaches and buses were laid on to take them off,' a young police officer informed her. 'They've all left now, of course, but I can arrange for a minibus to do the same for you.' His eye passed over the remaining group who nodded agreement. The minibus was ordered and they were soon climbing into it. Never had it felt so good to sit down and lean back and relax.

The group in front of Guy and Kate were saying that the tree must have been old and diseased to keel over as it had. 'It must have come down between the nine-thirty express and ours. Driver's dead so he can't give his version.'

'Life's chancy these days. Never know when you set off in the morning if you'll get home in one piece.'

'Or home at all.'

'True enough.'

Snippets of conversation like this continued to ricochet around in the bus as it sped towards Mark's Hill, the first stop after Royle's Cross. Kate and Guy contributed little. Half-asleep in their seat, they were disinclined to say much, least of all about the crash. Kate sat cuddled inside Guy's jacket, pressed against his shirt.

'I can't forget it for one single second,' she muttered once, 'but right now I wish they'd shut up about it.'

'I know…same here.' His chin grazed her forehead, stiff with stubble.

'We should have rung home,' she said presently.

'Better that we didn't. They'll probably think we've gone clubbing to round off the day. News of the crash won't be out until tomorrow's early news and papers.'

'Which is today.' Kate straightened and peered out of the window at the little town of Mark's Hill, its shops night-lit, its houses in darkness and, as it was Sunday, not even a friendly milkman whining around on his float. It was just a damp and deserted November morning that she was lucky to be seeing...that some people would *never* see.

Once again she felt her stomach sliding as she visualised that line of plastic-covered bodies laid out in the field. She remembered the child, she remembered the baby, and tears came then, silent tears that ran like rain down her face and onto Guy's hand.

'Don't, Kate...*don't Kate!*' He sounded angry as he heaved himself up on one hip to scrabble for his handkerchief, which he thrust into her hand.

'Keeps coming back...like indigestion!' She tried to laugh and failed.

'It's the same with me, but we *did* help—keep hanging onto that. We knew what to do, without too much telling. We must try to be glad about that and not keep going over it, tearing ourselves to bits.'

'You were fantastic.' She mopped and blew.

'You weren't so bad yourself.'

'Plaudits all round now, is it?' She laughed naturally this time, moving inside his jacket again. She slipped her arm round his waist, feeling him shift to fit her against him. Incredibly she slept.

He roused her when they were nearly at Grantford, where they were the last to be set down. Sitting up, she could see the bridge and the lights on its parapet. She shivered a little. Their driver was asking where they wanted to be set down, being the last two passengers.

Guy leaned forward to call out, 'To Riverstone Lodge in Guessens Road for Dr Burnett, then to Melbridge for me—Larchwood House Surgery. After which I've no doubt you'll be glad to get back to Royle's Cross.'

'I'm used to night work. Doesn't bother me, Doc,' he said as they crossed the bridge. 'I dare say you get your share of it too.'

'Now and again, yes, we do.' Guy moved to help Kate, who was searching around for her shoulder-bag, dragging it up from the floor.

Minutes later, in the porch at Riverstone, he unlocked the front door. 'I'll see you later on...drive over before lunch.'

'Yes, please do that.' She turned and pulled his head down to hers, and they kissed in a bumpy, clumsy fashion, both of them aware of the waiting minibus on the other side of the hedge.

Kate heard it drive off as she went in and shut the door. Merle came out from her bed in the kitchen and thrust a long nose into her hand, but she barked as well, rousing Laura who came out onto the landing. 'Nothing like coming home with the milk,' she yawned. 'Hope you had a good time. Whatever did you come in—it sounded like a bus?'

'It *was* a bus, well, sort of,' Kate said, climbing the stairs. Putting her arms around her mother, she told her about the crash, and Guy's and her part in it, emphasising their lucky escape. 'And, no, Mum, we're neither of us hurt so there's no need to look like that.'

Laura was shocked, but into action not torpor. She ran a bath for Kate, filled a hot-water bottle and brought her a whisky and milk toddy in bed. Resisting the urge to watch over her for the rest of the night, she went back to her own room, leaving both their doors ajar.

CHAPTER SIX

LAURA took a breakfast tray and two of the morning papers in to Kate at nine a.m. The train disaster featured widely in both papers. There was a list of those killed, and a centre spread of lurid pictures that appalled Kate all over again. She managed to hide her feelings from her mother who, she knew, wanted to go to church. She did most Sundays. She liked the morning service—it helped her cope with her week. 'I'll leave you to put the joint in.' Laura believed in regular meals. 'And it's pork so it'll need to go into a hot oven at eleven,' she said.

Kate's sleep had been the fitful kind, and breakfast was hard to get down but she managed it. Then she had another hot bath to ease her stiffness and bring out her bruises. As she lay back in the water, moving her legs up and down, she wondered about Guy—wondered if he, too, was discovering black and blue areas exquisitely tender to touch.

Pulling on jeans and an over-sized shirt which was comfortable to wear, she went downstairs to wave her mother off down the drive. As she washed up the breakfast things she thought about Guy again. They were on the brink of becoming lovers. Yesterday had brought them close, but for how long? He'd be gone soon, he'd more or less told her that.

'I don't think I could cope with a short affair,' she confided to a watchful Merle, who was hoping for left-over toast. She gave her usual bark when the doorbell shrilled. That would be Guy...almost certainly Guy!

Excitement leapt in Kate as she flung down the tea towel, restraining herself from running to the door.

He was there, he'd come, it was him. There he stood, smiling down at her. 'Am I too early?'

'Course not.' She stood back and let him in.

'Only I've got an errand to do for John—a set of chessmen to return to his friend in The Close so I thought as Riverstone was on my way…'

He looked so disarming, so disturbing in his fawn twills and Arran sweater, that she was speechless for a few seconds. Then she heard herself telling him that Laura was out, but that she was glad he'd come. They went into the sitting-room and sat together on the couch. She offered him coffee, but he shook his head. 'How are you this morning?' he asked.

'All right. Are you?' She swallowed and smiled.

'Yes, I'm pretty much the same. The papers are full of the crash, not that I've read them much yet.'

'No, I haven't either.'

She heard him sigh, then he took her hand, clasping it loosely in the space between them, caressing her palm with his thumb. 'You did sterling work last night, Dr Kate.'

'You were pretty good yourself.'

'We were good together.'

They turned to each other and Guy's arm slipped around her waist, drawing her against him—against his shoulder—as he'd done in the bus last night. This time she raised her face for his kiss. He smelled the fragrance of her hair…and her skin…and her breath, heard the sigh she gave.

'Oh, Kate!' He stroked her neck, running his fingers through her hair to the crown, bending her back and kissing her mouth. She exploded under his touch—under the magic of his lips which caressed like his hands—and she wanted him over her, and down on her, and inside her. Her body ached where he didn't touch. Then he sat up and put her from him, got up and went to the window, standing there with his back to her. She felt as though she'd been roused, then denied on purpose and hated him till she heard him say, 'I must go now...before I forget my manners.' This eased the atmosphere *and* the desperate feeling. It even made her laugh.

'Well, of course, if you feel like that!' she parried.

'I think you know full well what I feel like!' He pulled her up from the couch. 'But this isn't the right time or place, is it?'

With her blood settling at last, it was easy to shake her head and say no.

'So, come and see me off.' At the front door, just before he stepped out, he put his arms around her again. He enfolded her only, not crushing her to him, as he whispered into her ear. 'If you want me as much as I do you, we'll fix a time and place *soon*, won't we?' He tilted her face up to his.

'Yes, I think we must. Of course, we might go off during the waiting time!' She could tease him now, and he pretended to shake her. 'Speak for yourself,' he said, and strode towards the Rover, giving a toot as he drove off.

Heavens, that was close. Kate leaned against the inside of the door as she shut it, but he was right—it was the wrong time and place. Where would they eventually make love, as she now knew they would? It was like a die that had been cast. Nothing would stop them. The thought of this set Kate's pulses racing all over again, and she had to sit down at once.

She was in the hall, and when the phone rang it was practically in her ear. It would be a patient for sure, she thought, then remembered she wasn't on call. Neither was Guy until midnight. Graingers were covering till then. It could be Uncle John...probably was. She lifted the receiver, getting the shock of her life within seconds of announcing her name...

'Kate, this is Mike.'

The shock was so great that she couldn't speak at first, just sank on the chair again. He was calling her name, over and over. 'Kate, Kate, are you there?'

'Of course, I'm just surprised, that's all.' She managed to steady her voice. 'Are you ringing from Boston? It'll cost a bomb.'

'No, I'm in England, and I'm ringing to ask if you're all right. I saw you getting on the late train at Waterloo last night, then this morning I read...saw about the crash, and I wondered if—'

'I'm fine, just fine.' Yet even as she spoke she wondered if she was for the hall flooring—a shiny parquet—seemed to be climbing the walls. 'How did you know...?' She swallowed, then went on. 'How did you know where I was?'

'They told me at Mamesbury. I went there when I first came home. The receptionist at your old practice told me that you'd gone into partnership with your uncle and were living at home. I've been back six weeks. I've left America for good. I'm living at Fulham for the time being.'

'I see,' Kate said faintly, trying to take all this in. How many times had she fantasised about Mike coming back...coming back for good and getting in touch with her?

'Can we meet?' he was saying, even more amazingly. 'Can I come and see you now? I'm in Grantford at The Bridge Hotel. I drove down from Fulham as soon as I'd seen the paper. I do want to see you, Kate.'

He was that close. He was in Grantford. Surely she

was dreaming all this. 'If you want to come, do so.' She forced herself to be cool because—even counting that he'd said he was worried about her—he still had a nerve to get in touch with no warning after all this time. What had happened to Caroline Ellenburgh? Had he walked out on her too, or was she over here with him, all hair and glasses and calling England ''quaint''?

After a careful look in the kitchen mirror she stood by the sink, sipping a glass of water till she saw a white Peugeot stop at the entrance gates, then nose itself up the drive. Her glass went down on the draining-board with a click. Mike was getting out, thin, leggy, fair-haired, looking just the same. He looked about him and locked the car, his hair falling forward. He had it longer, and was wearing a suit, the jacket flying open as he straightened and came towards the house.

He had seen her at the window so he made for the kitchen door, which she had open before he could ring, standing back for him to come in. She smiled with dry lips, but was speechless as he was at first. Both spoke at once in a jumble of sound. They laughed and even that sounded strained, as though each was trying too hard.

'Come through and sit down.' Kate led the way into the sitting-room on feet that stumbled and legs that surely ended at the knees. She was the first to speak again as they sat down in facing chairs. 'I'd suggest a drink but perhaps, as you're driving...'

He shook his head, pushing back his hair. 'Nothing for me, thanks,' he said. 'I had coffee at the hotel as soon as I reached there.'

'You've had a long drive.'

'An hour and a half, not too bad. Kate, are you really all right? I mean, the crash...when I saw the papers.' He spread out his hands, palms uppermost, in a gesture she remembered, and emotion sluiced over her.

'As you see, I'm fine...' she smiled brightly '...bar a bruise or two. We were in the rear of the train. We'd nearly missed it so we had to get on where we could.'

'Good job you didn't walk up to the front after you got in.'

'I know. I've thought that a dozen times because we very nearly did.' Keep talking, keep talking, keep saying things! Her face ached from trying to smile.

'It was Guy Shearer, wasn't it—the bloke you were with?' Mike sounded as strained as she.

'Yes, it was Guy. We'd been to his father's wedding, and made a day of it.'

'I suppose he was over here for the wedding?'

'Not really, no. He's finished his post in Africa and he's working in the practice.'

Mike's eyes, pale blue and long-lashed, fluttered in surprise. 'So, you're a three-partner practice?'

'No, two—Guy's the locum. Uncle John was involved in a car accident back in the summer. He had a broken arm and ribs and a whiplash injury. Added to this, he was depressed over Dad. He needed to be off work.'

'Your Mamesbury practice told me about your father. I'm terribly sorry, Kate.' Mike inclined his head towards her almost supplicatingly. 'I'd have written if I'd known.'

'Really? I wonder why?' Kate's brows rose in disbelief. Shock was giving place to a curling anger. How *dare* he get in touch, for whatever reason, after all this time, after all he'd done?

'Of course I would have written. I liked your father.'

'Yes, I know, and he liked you too.' She swallowed, calming herself, hearing him ask about her mother. 'She's at church at the moment. She'll be sorry to have missed you.' What a terrible falsehood that was for her mother had had reservations about Mike, calling him an opportunist—whatever that might mean. Clearly, Mike had thought that Caroline and America were opportunities to be grasped quickly, without warning, in a single cut—like the slam of a butcher's cleaver.

Once again Kate was burning with outrage, which gave her the impetus to ask why he'd come back home after only eighteen months. 'I understood you were off to make a new life for good and all,' she reminded him deliberately, watching his colour come up.

'I should never have gone. I made a mistake.' He moved forward in his chair towards her, his eyes on her face, narrowed and blinking hard. This, she thought, is why he'd come down here. He wants to confess all…to someone…to me, who'll say "no harm done" and make him feel comfortable and good about himself again, as I always used to do.

Well, I won't, and that's that. He deserves a kick for what he did to me. All she said was, 'Oh, dear, I'm sorry.' She allowed her gaze to wander towards the window, and through it into the garden, where she spotted Guy, getting out of the Rover and staring across at Mike's car. Why had he come back, and so soon?

'Oh, here's Guy!' She sprang to her feet. 'You'll be able to meet him again.'

'Mike's turned up,' she said, as soon as she'd got the door open.

Guy looked stunned, did a double take and then marched through and shook Mike's hand. 'You on leave?' he asked, which was a fair question.

'No, back for good. The American fast lane and their junk diet didn't agree with me,' Mike replied with a forced grin, reseating himself.

'Got a job lined up, have you?' Guy took the chair opposite.

'Lined up, but not landed yet. I've only been back six weeks. I'm on the short-list for two so, with a bit of luck…' He made another of his sweeping gestures, going on to ask if Guy intended to go abroad again.

'Possibly, yes, I enjoy the challenge,' Guy said offhandedly, a remark not lost on Kate who was looking over at the two men from her seat on the sofa. Their dissimilarity was marked. Mike, tall and narrowly built, was elegant in a suit. Guy was just as tall but burly, and as dark as Mike was fair, dressed for comfort in his twills and sweater. Yesterday had been suit-time for him, as it had for her. Picking a thread of cotton off her trousers, she made room for Merle on the couch.

Guy asked where Mike was living, and was told, 'Staying with an old student friend. You remember Tom, don't you, Kate?' He smiled across at her.

'Of course,' she said, but her voice shook a little. Memories were dangerous things. Tom Baker belonged to the happy times. He'd often come to Wiltshire to visit his parents and had sometimes stayed a night at the flat.

'I was telling Kate…' Mike went on in the quick, light voice that reminded her of so many things—of whispered confidences, of excited exchanges. 'I was telling Kate that I saw you both boarding the train last night. I was coming back from visiting my folks in Hampshire and glimpsed you, making your dash.'

'So he came here this morning to make sure we were both in the land of the living.' Kate half laughed, then caught herself because the silly, unthinking words brought back images of long shapes, being laid out in that horrible field. The whole crash scenario swung back—the sights and sounds and smells. She felt cold and nauseous and tried to brace herself, catching her bottom lip in her teeth.

'Neither of us,' Guy was saying, 'got very much sleep last night.' She could scarcely hear him...scarcely hear him... He was fading, fading away. She supposed she cried out or made some sort of sign for suddenly Guy was close, bending right over her and pushing her head between her knees till all she could see was the carpet between her feet and the white rim of her trainers. Her middle felt folded up. 'Keep her like that,' he was instructing Mike. 'I've got a flask in the car. I won't be a minute!' Out he went. Kate felt the draught from the door. She wanted to stop him, tell him not to bother, but by then he was back with a tot of medicinal brandy in a beaker she'd left on the draining-board.

'I don't want it.' She pushed at it, the smell assaulting her nose.

'No arguments. Gulp it down quickly—that way it'll do the most good.'

She did as he said. He was still standing close, and she knew that if she resisted he was perfectly capable of nipping her nose and force-feeding her.

As the brandy hit the back of her throat and she felt its glow going down, she felt instantly steadier. She even managed to laugh at Mike who stood by Guy's side, looking stunned. 'I'm perfectly all right,' she told them both. 'You don't need to stand there like the dreaded men in white coats!'

'Are you sure?' Guy asked.

'I'm sure.'

'Well, in that case...' he moved back '...I feel I ought to be going. Ma's got guests for lunch, and you two will have a lot to talk about. No, please don't get up...either of you. I know the way to the door!' And with that he was gone. Presently they saw the car, moving off down the drive.

'Would you like me to get you a glass of water?' Mike was still looking alarmed, which wasn't surprising. In the old days Kate had not been the fainting kind.

'No, I'm all right. The brandy's done the trick. Guy's methods usually work!'

'He doesn't change much, does he?'

Kate bridled a little. 'I can't see that he needs to,' she said. 'He's abrupt, I know, and a bit bossy, but he's brave and he gets things done.'

'What's he like to work with?' Mike crossed his legs and leaned back.

'Fine, just fine, and the patients like him. He'll be gone, though, in the New Year.' Kate was wishing he hadn't gone off now, not quite so suddenly. Alone with Mike she felt all at sea. Why had he come? If he'd wondered about the train crash he could have rung her from Fulham, and why wait six whole weeks, before getting in touch with her? Perhaps because of Caroline. Perhaps she was also in Fulham.

Until she knew more, understood more, she'd feel wary and ill at ease. In the end she played safe by asking him about the two jobs he'd been short-listed for. He was plainly glad to tell her.

'One of them's at the Walbrook,' he said.

'Now that's *brilliant*!' She was impressed and showed that she was.

'The other is at a private clinic at Asterleigh Park. Out of the two of them I'd like to land that one. Now that I'm out of the NHS I'd quite like to stay that way.'

'Asterleigh Park's not far from here. I've heard Uncle mention the Redlands Clinic. I expect that's the one you mean.'

'Yes, and if I get it I shall have to live down this way,' he said, looking straight at her.

Quickly, she asked, 'Which interview comes first?'

'The Walbrook one is tomorrow, Redlands on Tuesday.'

'What a harrowing week.'

'Yes, I'm dreading it,' he said, and that wasn't a pose. He had never been conceited, Kate remembered, or even overly confident. He had always said she'd given him confidence, made him walk tall. Maybe Caroline Ellenburgh had failed in that quarter. It took knack and tact and love and patience to polish a man's ego.

It was on the tip of her tongue to ask him about Caroline, but somehow the words wouldn't come. Instead she smiled and wished him luck. 'I'll keep my fingers crossed for you,' she said.

His reaction to that was swift. 'Please do—it'll make all the difference to me. I've missed you, Kate.' His voice grew urgent. 'I've missed you so much!'

'That's nice,' she said lightly, hearing, as she did so, her mother's key scraping in the lock. 'That'll be Mother, back from church.'

'Oh, great!' Mike shot to his feet just as Laura entered the room and stared at him in disbelief.

'Well, now, you're the very last person I expected to see in my lounge,' she said perfectly pleasantly but un-smilingly, and Kate hurried to explain.

'Mike saw Guy and me getting on the train last night. He wondered if we were all right. He's driven down from Fulham.'

'You're on leave, are you?' Laura stripped off her gloves while Mike explained, all over again, that he was home for good. 'You must have had a short contract.' Laura didn't sit down, which effectively meant that Mike couldn't either. In the end Kate hurried to tell her mother that he'd got to get back to Town.

'That's true, I have, so I'll say goodbye.' He put out a tentative hand which, to Kate's relief, her mother took.

'Safe journey back,' she said, still unsmilingly, then she made her way upstairs.

'Come out with me and have a look at my car.' Mike took Kate's arm. 'I only got it yesterday, through a friend of Tom's.'

'So far,' she said, as they went down the steps, 'you've not done so badly since you came back from the States. You've got somewhere to live, two interviews lined up and now a nearly new car. It looks straight off the production line, doesn't it?' She slid in as he unlocked its door.

'Will you make my good luck continue, by agreeing to see me again?' He was peering in at her, bent almost double, which made his face look strained. 'Will you give me a chance to tell you why I acted as I did?'

'I already know why.' Kate settled herself behind the steering-wheel. 'You got fed up with our life together so made one with someone else.'

'I was led by the nose.'

'It's called "enticed" in the divorce courts, I believe, but, of course, we weren't married, were we? Where's Caroline now?' she asked in almost the same breath, hearing him draw in his own.

'At her home in Boston. Things went wrong between us. We tried, but it didn't work out.'

'I'm glad you tried.' She couldn't quite manage to keep the jibe out of her voice.

'I suppose I deserved that.'

'Fully!' She peered into the glove compartment, her hair falling forward over her face, her thoughts rioting. So Caroline Ellenburgh hadn't been able to make him happy. He wants me back—that's why he's here, that's why he's come, that's why he went down to Mamesbury to find me. It could all happen again between him and me…but do I want it to?

'We can meet again if you want, Mike…' she began to get out of the car '…but we can't slot back to the way we once were. Too much has happened since then.'

'I don't expect anything…only to see you.' He looked flustered and hot. His hands were deep in his pockets, spoiling the line of his perfect suit.

'If you give me Tom's number, I'll ring you,' she suggested. 'That would be the best way, I think.'

'Can't we fix something now?' His face blanked.

'No, I don't think we can, but if you give me the number I *will* ring. I'm not playing silly games.' A motorbike roared by in the road, all but drowning her words, but Mike had heard her. She could tell by his frown and the little nod he gave.

'If you want to do it that way round, fine.' He dived into the car, found a scrap of paper, scribbled on it and handed it over to her.

As she glanced at it, thanking him, she felt him moving in close. 'I'll ring you Tuesday evening,' she said, 'and chance you being in.'

'I'll be in.' He bent to kiss her, but she drew away, laughing and shaking her head. 'We have nosy neighbours—no need to give them a treat!'

'Right.' He looked hurt and got into the car. Kate swallowed, hating herself.

'Remember me to Tom, and good luck with the interviews. I'm glad you came,' she added, bending to the level of the car window. She received a smile and a word of thanks in return before he drove away.

God, that had been tricky! Stiff with nerves, Kate

hugged herself in the chill wind, before turning and going back into the house.

'Well, that was a turn-up for the book!' Laura said, meeting her in the hall. Kate followed her into the kitchen.

'I was totally shocked when he phoned!'

'Oh, he did ring first, then, not just appear?'

'*Mum*!'

'Oh, all right, sorry... Has he got a job?'

'Not yet, but he's applied for several. He's got interviews this week. He's a senior physio with a good track record so he's bound to get one of them.'

Laura tied on her striped apron, bringing the strings round to the front. 'What about that girl he swanned off with?'

'They didn't get on, they've parted and, before you ask, yes, I am seeing him again—that's what he wants.'

'I'm sure he does.' Laura's tone was expressive, and it flicked Kate on the raw.

'There's no need to be sarky,' she flared. 'I know you don't like Mike!'

'That's not true, I do,' Laura averred, then spoiled it by adding, 'But, then, I like most people so it's not much of a compliment. What I didn't like, what I deplored, was his cavalier treatment of you. Was Guy here when he telephoned?'

'No, he slipped out to do an errand for Uncle, but he came back when Mike was still here. He didn't stay long, though. Sylvia had guests for lunch.'

'Oh, really!' Laura sounded abstracted. 'Talking about lunch,' she continued, 'you forgot to put the pork in— not that I'm surprised, with all that's been going on here this morning.'

Kate clapped a hand to her mouth. 'Oh, Mummy, I'm sorry!'

'Never mind, don't make a fuss. It's not worth it, for heaven's sake. We'll have soup and cheese and biscuits now, then cook the pig tonight!' She poured the soup into a saucepan and bore it to the cooker, stirring it with unnecessary vigour. She admitted to herself that, despite her avowal that she liked Mike Merrow, she could have wished him in outer space.

CHAPTER SEVEN

IT WAS Laura who answered the telephone at a little before four o'clock, calling to Kate who was coming in after a meditative walk, 'It's Guy, darling, he wants to know if you're free to speak. I told him Mike had cleared off, which I'm sure was what he meant.'

'Oh, good.' Kate was glad he'd rung. She'd been hoping that he would. She was anxious to know why he'd come back that morning just after Mike had turned up. 'Guy, hello.' She pulled off her headscarf, and sat on the hall chair, telling him in reply to his enquiry that she was perfectly all right. 'I haven't had any more attacks of the vapours. I wouldn't dare, not with Mum about!'

He didn't mention Mike, but went on to tell her why he'd rung. 'It's about Sue Avers, Kate, or, rather, about her husband. John's chess-playing friend pointed out to me, when I was at his house this morning, that Clive Avers's name appeared on the list of those killed in the crash.'

'Oh, good Lord! Oh, Guy... Oh, no!' Kate sprang up from the chair. 'I'll go and see her now, at once. Oh, how awful... Oh, poor Sue! How could I possibly have missed that name. I did read the list so how could I possibly have missed it? I'll get the car out and drive round now.'

'I'd like to come with you,' Guy interrupted, 'unless, of course, you feel that two of us turning up would be a bit much.'

'No, I don't. I don't think that at all. I'm sure Sue

92

would like to see you. She lives nearer you than I do so shall I come and pick you up?'

'I'll pick you up.' Guy's tone was firm. 'You've had enough to contend with today.'

It was getting dark when the Rover came nosing up the drive at a little after four. Kate slipped in beside Guy. 'I've since looked in the paper,' she said, 'and seen Clive's name. I don't know how I came to miss it earlier. I couldn't have been concentrating.'

'That wouldn't surprise me, after the night we had.' He did a three-point turn in the drive, making the gravel spray. 'I knew when I called the second time this morning, but felt the time wasn't exactly appropriate to mention it then.'

'You mean, with Mike there?' Kate introduced his name deliberately.

'Yes, and with you as pale as your shirt.' He eased the car into the road. 'It must have been a shock, having him turn up like that.'

'I'm feeling it now. I still can't believe it. I can't seem to grasp that he's here, that I'm not dreaming it... It all seems so unreal.'

'I can see that it must.' They approached the roundabout, then turned off to the left. Kate expected him to ask more about Mike, but he seemed disinclined to talk about anything other than their impending meeting with Sue. 'She'll have to take compassionate leave,' he said, after a reflective silence. 'We can't expect her to turn up next week and take her clinics as usual.'

'No, of course not. We'll just have to manage between us. Sue's part time, as you know, and if we can't mop up three days between us it's a pretty poor do.'

Guy nodded. Kate caught the movement. They were approaching the bridge, but once down on the other side he began to slacken speed. Kate thought she knew why.

They weren't far from Sue's house, and it was one of those times when it was infinitely better to travel than to arrive. She felt the same reluctance to a certain extent. Sue wasn't a patient but a colleague and friend, which made all the difference in the world. And Guy liked Sue. The two had a rapport—Kate had noticed it before.

They saw the house as soon as they turned into Beech Avenue—the second one down in a pair of semi-detached. There were lights on in both downstairs and upstairs windows, and as the Rover drew up at the kerb the front door opened and a middle-aged couple came out, turning to wave to Sue who was standing on the steps. When she saw the car she stayed where she was, outlined against the hall light—a small figure in a dark dress, straining to see who else she had to be polite to at the end of a long and melancholy day.

'I've had loads of visitors,' she called out, as she recognised Kate and Guy, 'but it's good to see *you*.' She let them into a narrow hall, carpeted in fawn and smelling strongly of the chrysanthemums that splayed out from a tall bronze urn. 'From the vicar,' Sue said carelessly, touching one of the blooms. 'He probably took them off the font—or robbed someone's grave.'

True to form, she's determined to joke, Kate thought, and wished she wouldn't. Through in a small, over-warm sitting-room was a girl younger than Sue, but so similar in looks that she had to be a relative. She was reading to Sue's little girls. 'Meet my sister, Iris,' Sue said. 'Now, brats…' She bent down to the girls. 'Iris is going to give you your tea—at least, I *think* she is.'

'Too right, I am.' Iris took the hint. She marshalled the children and went out, closing the door behind her. Kate and Guy sat down.

'We're so sorry, Sue.' Guy spoke first. 'It's a terrible time for you.'

'It was a terrible crash—a tree on the line—but you'll have seen that from the papers.' Sue seated herself on a pouffe, looking at neither of them.

Kate took a deep breath, and said, 'Guy and I were on the train, Sue. We got on right at the end. Our carriage didn't tip over and we were able to get out. It was the front that bore the brunt. We stayed on to help the rescue teams, and were there all night.'

Sue's face became animated for the first time. 'You stayed to help, then… Did you see Clive, see him being got out? You know him, don't you?' She looked straight at Kate. 'Did you see him alive?'

'We saw no one we knew, Sue,' Guy put in quietly. 'There were several teams of rescuers and a great deal of…chaos. It wasn't possible to pick anyone out.'

'They told me he died in the ambulance—he had chest injuries. He was taken to St Mark's. I saw him this morning— Iris came with me. He looked peaceful, remote. I expect the funeral will be on Friday.' Sue got up and knelt on the hearthrug to turn up the gas fire. 'I can't get this place warm somehow, yet the heating's been on all day.'

'You're to take some leave,' Kate told her gently.

'I'll only need tomorrow as there'll be things to arrange, and then, of course, Friday. But I'll be at the surgery on Wednesday, and the week after that I'll be doing my usual three days. I don't want to put you out.'

'Don't push yourself, Sue.'

'Do I ever?' A ghost of Sue's normal grin showed on her face for a second as she answered Kate.

'And if there's anything we can do, anything at all, let us know,' Guy said. 'I'm glad you've got your sister with you.'

'Yes, she'll help with the kids so I can get on with the arrangements.' Sue rose to pull the curtains over the window. She didn't reseat herself and, taking this as a sign that she wanted to be left on her own, Kate and Guy also got to their feet.

As they went out into the floral-smelling hall again they could see the two little girls through in the kitchen, having boiled eggs for their tea. To Kate's surprise Guy crossed over and went in to them.

'Those look good. I like brown eggs,' he addressed the elder girl.

'They're free-range,' she informed him importantly. 'Mummy never buys any others.'

'And we've got jelly for afters,' Emily, the three-year-old, said through a mouthful of toast. 'Daddy makes it wibble and wobble, and once it fell *on the floor*!'

Both children went into paroxysms of laughter. At five and three years old respectively, accidents were fun.

'They don't know yet—I haven't told them,' Sue said at the front door. 'I just can't find the words at the moment. I'll try again tomorrow.'

'The sooner the better.' Kate gave her a hug. 'Young though they are, they still have to know.'

'I know, and I'll do it. Thanks for coming,' Sue said, as Guy kissed her cheek.

'Nice kids,' he remarked to Kate, as they set off for home. She looked at him curiously.

'I thought you said you didn't like children.'

'No, *you* said that,' he pointed out. In the next breath he went on to say that John had informed him that Sue's marriage to Clive hadn't been the made-in-heaven sort.

'To put it even more strongly, it was a marriage from hell. Sue unburdened herself to me once,' Kate replied. 'Clive had a long-standing girlfriend in Town. He and Sue lived separate lives, although he never left home— probably for the sake of the children, who thought the world of him.'

'Still…' Guy dropped speed a little as they passed the war memorial '…even if there was little or no love lost, it must be hard for Sue now. Presumably they were happy once.'

'Yes, they must have been. As you say, she must be feeling rough now. I feel so sorry for her.'

'So do I, but maybe now she'll have a chance to find happiness.'

'Not so easy, with two small children.'

'Maybe not. Anyway, how about you and Merrow— I suppose he wants you back again?' Guy flicked a glance at her and she stiffened.

'There's nothing like *asking*,' she said.

'I think I'm entitled to do so, bearing in mind that you and I were about to embark on a sexual relationship.'

She drew in her breath. 'There was nothing agreed.'

'Oh, really? I thought there was, but now you're thrown by Merrow's reappearance, aren't you? You want me to take a back seat.'

'Why must you be so…be so aggressive? I had no idea Mike would come back!' she defended angrily, staring at his face which showed no expression at all, He made no reply either, but slowed the car and pulled in near the bridge. 'We'll get out and walk for a bit,' he said, without consulting her. She heard the handbrake ratchet—fiercely, like a neck being wrung—then he was out of the car and already on the towpath before she could gather her wits.

When Kate caught up with him he took her arm and drew her close to his side but only to avoid a cyclist, riding along with no lights. Next they met a giggling couple, then an old man with a dog. After that he relinquished her arm, and they plodded on, side by side like inveterate walkers, their feet making rustling sounds.

It was dark in the sense that darkness had fallen, but

they could see well enough by the lamps on the bridge they had left behind and from reflected lights, spilling out from houses on the opposite bank.

'We're down here to talk about Mike, aren't we?' Kate ventured to ask after they'd been walking for several minutes, with nothing being said. 'In answer to your question about whether he wants me back again, I think perhaps he does, but all I've done so far is agree to see him again.'

'How did he know where you were living? Did he just guess last night when he saw us at the station that you were back with your folks?'

'He got the information from a friend of mine at Pritchard's, my old practice. He went to the flat first to find me—'

'Expecting to find you still there, beavering away, eating your heart out for him? What an ego the man must have!'

'I don't agree! I think him going there made a lot of sense. I mean, if Dad hadn't died, and if Uncle John hadn't come up with the partnership, I might have still been there—''beavering away'', as you call it. A girl has to eat! And Mike's not egotistical—that's the *last* thing he is.'

'All right, you know him better than I do.'

'Yes.' Kate's voice was small. They were very nearly quarrelling, and she hated it. The reason came to her out of the dark…she was on the brink of falling in love with him, which would be disastrous because he'd be gone in a matter of weeks. It couldn't be love—it had to be just body chemistry. She stumbled and Guy caught her arm.

'I take it he's left his American love on the other side of the Atlantic?' He let go of her arm and put his hands in his pockets, hunching away from her.

'Things didn't work out for him,' she said defensively.
'Obviously not.'

His scoffing tone maddened her. 'Well, don't rubbish him,' she flared. 'He made a mistake—a big one, it's true—but it can happen to the best of us!'

'You're very forgiving!'

'And you're being nasty!'

A twig cracked under his foot. 'Yes,' he admitted, 'thoroughly nasty.'

'And I'm cold.' Kate spun on her heel. 'Surely we've walked far enough.'

'You should have said.' Guy turned, stripped off his jacket and laid it over her shoulders, all but dropping it there. He was careful not to touch her, and she felt a chill of a different kind.

'I didn't mean...' She made to take it off, but he stopped her and held it in place.

'It's not just my coat you're shrugging off, is it? Merrow's return has thrown and confused you and you don't know which way to jump. If he's the one you want—and perhaps in the long term he's the best choice—then you must tell me so, not play with us both, like juggling two bloody balls!'

'You'll be gone at Christmas.' It was all she could think of to say, and he actually laughed.

'And that, I think, is my answer. Come on, let's get back to the car. We're both rocking on our feet. The best thing we can do is get home to bed...not together, of course.' He was sneering now. 'You've decided to re-nege on that!'

Later that night Kate decided that all he'd wanted had been a short, sharp, feisty affair, with no hard feelings at the end of it. She also faced the fact that he was an attractive, deeply passionate man. She was sure he'd find

someone else to suit him, someone light-hearted and fun
who wouldn't want to cling when the time came to part
and who wasn't related to him, not even by marriage,
so there'd be no family looking on.

After such a chaotic weekend it seemed extraordinary to
find everything looking as usual in the surgery next day.
When Kate went in she found Guy in the office, checking through Sue's appointments. He asked for her help
and they went over them together, deciding which
should be cancelled and enlisting the help of Dr John
who was anxious to be involved.

There was nothing in Guy's manner to embarrass or
discomfit her. In fact, his very normality as the morning
wore on caused her the tiniest pinprick of disappointment, even of mild outrage. Was this going to be his
attitude from now on—pleasant but impersonal?

They met in the treatment room several times, and
once he enlisted her help when a new patient, an eighty-
five-year-old woman, objected to him syringing her ears.
'My appointment was with the nurse,' she insisted. 'I
don't want a man touching my ears so if *you* can't do
it…' she glared at Kate '…I'll wait till another day!'

'If you'll just hang on for five minutes, Mrs Wearham,
I'll come back and do them for you,' Kate said, hearing
Guy leave the room. She had been in the middle of listening to a patient's chest, and the poor man, with his
vest hitched up, was waiting for her to finish. He was
good about it, though, and didn't complain. 'You'll be
lost without Nurse,' he said. 'Sad about her husband,
wasn't it? Terrible shock for her.'

There had been a lot of talk about Sue in the waiting-
room.

'Makes you realise the amount of work Sue takes off

us,' Guy remarked, when surgery was over at last and Meg was locking the doors.

'Sue's well liked. Everyone was asking about her,' Kate replied. 'Patients often prefer to see her—she has more time to listen to them.'

'I didn't make much impact on the elderly Mrs Wearham.' Guy pulled a wry face.

'No, your charm didn't work for once,' Kate said tartly, and immediately wished she hadn't for he gave her a long, measuring look that put her in her place. Dr John, lost in thoughts of his own and impervious to atmosphere, smiled at them both, unhooking the stethoscope from his neck.

'Those few patients I saw were a tonic. They made me realise how much I'd miss practising if I retired early,' he said, opening the door into the link passage and going through into the house. His arm, now out of plaster, was supported in a light sling, his ribs had healed, and although his neck injury still gave him trouble he wore his collar for shorter periods and discarded it when he went out.

'He'll be good and ready to see the back of me come Christmas,' Guy remarked, sitting in the chair John had vacated and pulling some papers towards him.

'Well, you've still got another six weeks to go,' Kate said to the back of his head.

'Been counting them, have you?' He swivelled to face her, and in doing so knocked against the cup of coffee on his desk and sent its contents streaming over his blotter and papers.

'Damn it to hell!' He leapt to his feet to escape the sticky brown flow. Kate shot out to fetch a cloth, and returned to find that he'd swept the papers onto the carpet, still swearing under his breath.

'There may not be much harm done.' Kate mopped

the desk top and inside an open drawer, then she got clean tissues and dabbed at the papers, putting them by the radiator to dry. 'There you are.' She sat back on her heels. 'That's not so bad... With a clean blotter and a spray of polish, all will be cured.'

'That was quick work—thank you.' He didn't reseat himself. 'It must be the effect you have on me because I'm not usually clumsy,' he added, watching her rise to her feet, soggy tissues in hand. He took them from her, tossed them in the bin then turned to face her again. 'What a pity it is,' he said, looking down at the crown of her golden head, 'that we can't clear up our own little problem with a clean blotter and a polish spray.'

Kate raised startled eyes to his. He looked totally serious. 'Well, isn't it?' he insisted gently, touching the point of her chin.

'I suppose so.' She wanted him to kiss her.

'You *know* so but, of course, we don't really want to be cured, do we?' His hand smoothed the curve of her neck down past the chunky edge of her bob and forward to her throat. At that moment a tap at the door made them spring apart and Enid entered, staring in horror at the paper-strewn floor.

'Oh, Doctor, an accident...all over the carpet, too!' Under cover of her fussing Kate made a wise but unwilling exit from the room.

Ten minutes later, driving down the high street *en route* to the first of her calls, she told herself that her and Guy's little problem was a simple case of sex. It could be cured quite simply by avoidance. I'm so muddled by Mike coming back. I loved him once, *really* loved him—not just fancied him. There's no future with Guy. There can't be—he'd said that himself.

Prior to evening surgery her uncle suggested that it

might be a good idea to take Sue Avers out to lunch one day. 'After the funeral, naturally.'

'Splendid idea, John. Make her feel valued.' Guy was quick to agree. 'Shall we leave it to you to mention it to her?'

'No, you can do it, or Kate can. Make it some time next week.' John looked thoughtfully at the two of them as he finished his tea.

Evening surgeries were mainly attended by the younger, working patients. Kate's five o'clock patient was a young woman of thirty, who was complaining of tiredness. 'It's ever since I had my appendix out, Doctor. I had it done at the General on a day-surgery basis. There were no complications and I went back to work after a month.

'I'm still working, or trying to, but I'm so slow that I can't get through what I should. I sit in front of my computer and although I know what I want to input I can't seem to hack it out of my brain. It's like ploughing through a fog. The effort slays me, and when I get home at night I've hardly got the energy to lift a kettle, let alone cook a meal.'

Kate gave her a general check-up, took venous blood for a count, asked for a urine specimen and checked her blood pressure and pulse. 'I don't expect to find anything wrong, Miss Anderson... Yes, you can pull your sleeve down now. The symptoms you describe are what we call post-operative fatigue. You have to remember that although you were in and out of hospital in a matter of hours you had a full general anaesthetic.

'Now, that affects people in different ways. Some bounce back to normal and regain their energy quickly, but many are like you—they feel tired, lethargic, heavy and miserable, and they don't know why they do. They become anxious, which makes them even more tired.'

Kate looked sympathetically at the drawn, young face opposite her. 'Now,' she went on, 'is there any possibility of you being able to cut down your working hours for another couple of months to enable you to gain ground?'

'Well, actually...' Faith Anderson smiled for the first time '...I work for Mr Perry, the estate agent, who must be very fed up with me, but he *did* suggest I work mornings only, at least for a time, while we're in our slack season. Of course it'll mean a reduction in pay, but if you think that would be the answer I'd better take it up.'

'I would if I were you.' Kate returned her smile.

'So, no magic pills today, then?'

'I don't think you need them.' Kate laughed. As she watched Faith button her coat and reach down for her bag she recalled having caught a glimpse of her in the inner room at Perry's.

After Faith Anderson came a mother and daughter, the latter a child of twelve suffering from anaemia due to heavy periods. Kate prescribed an iron tonic and explained to the girl that quite often menorrhagia wasn't uncommon at the start of puberty.

A middle-aged man with a cough came next. There were always coughs, even in spring and summer. Chest complaints were the English disease. Taking her stethoscope out of her ears for the tenth time that day, Kate wrote out a prescription for an antibiotic, counselling Mr Priest to be sure to complete the ten-day course. 'Even if you think you're better, keep taking the tablets, please, and if you don't feel right in two weeks' time come back and see me again.'

'Wears you out, a cough does, Doctor.'

'It can be very troublesome,' Kate agreed, sounding her buzzer for the next patient—a builder with a lump in his groin.

*   *   *

It was over at last. The waiting room was empty, the street doors closed. Enid Ford was putting the notes away and Guy, in his room, was talking on the phone to one of the partners at Graingers. Kate heard him say, 'Yes, Peter... Sure, we can meet. Let me just check my diary.' After that she heard nothing because Sylvia came through from the house to ask how she was after the train disaster.

'What a mercy you were late getting on, and weren't sitting at the front. My blood runs cold, thinking about it!' In true theatrical form, she raised horrified eyes to the ceiling while Kate agreed with her.

She didn't see Guy before she left. She glanced at his door as she passed, but found it firmly closed with an aura of 'do not disturb' about it. Stifling disappointment, for she would have liked to compare notes with him about their action-packed day, she forced herself out into the yard and over to her car.

No sooner was she home than her mother told her Mike had telephoned. 'He said he'd ring later. He wants to tell you about his Walbrook interview—he sounded excited.'

'The arrangement was that I'd ring him tomorrow,' Kate said, going upstairs. She felt out of patience because she was tired, but when Mike rang again, just after supper, she tried to sound eager to hear his news.

'It's not in the bag, Kate, by any means,' he told her carefully, 'but I felt the panel—and one of them was Sir Courtney Blanche, the consultant in charge of the physio department—warmed to me—you know how it is. I don't think my interlude in America did me any harm. In fact, I think it improved my chances so it was just as well I went.'

It wasn't the fact that you went but the manner of your going, Kate could have said at this point but refrained. What was the use? If he liked to turn what he'd told her yesterday had been a terrible mistake into a sensible career move, then so be it, she thought. 'When do you think you'll hear for certain?' she asked him quietly, and was told in about a week.

'I've got the Redlands one tomorrow, of course. I'll be in Asterleigh Park by half-nine for the interview at ten.'

'I'll be thinking about you and I'll ring you, as promised, tomorrow evening.' As she spoke she could see her mother, coming out of the kitchen with two steaming cups of coffee which she was taking into the lounge.

She longed to be off the phone and drinking it, and felt guilty when Mike said, 'It's so good to be back, Kate, good to be able to tell you things again.'

'Thanks for the compliment,' she said lightly, feeling unaccountably embarrassed. The truth was that she felt awkward with him, didn't quite know how to *be*. She had to keep reminding herself that it really was Mike, the man to whom at one time she had confided all her secrets. It didn't do to be as open and trusting as that, she thought as she put down the phone.

During the two days that followed Mike was offered the Redlands post but not the Walbrook one. The Redlands committee offered him theirs on the day of the interview and he accepted it straight away, telling Kate he'd see her on Friday. His self-esteem was high.

Friday was the day on which Kate and Dr John were to attend Clive Avers's funeral. Guy wasn't able to be away from the surgery, and as Kate and her uncle knew Sue best it was decided that they should go so off they set in the Rover just after ten a.m.

Mike was at Riverstone when Kate got home to lunch. He had driven over from Asterleigh Park and was sitting in the kitchen with her mother while she laid the table for lunch. They seemed to be getting on all right. There was no sticky atmosphere, Kate was glad to notice, but perhaps her normal sensitivity had been blunted by funeral gloom. Mike had been looking over Redlands, she learned. He would start there in two weeks' time.

Laura asked him to lunch and the three of them ate cheese omelettes and fruit salad in the comfortably warm kitchen. 'We don't,' Laura explained, 'make much of lunch because of Kate having to get out on her afternoon calls.'

'Can I come with you?' he asked when Kate was due to set off. 'I don't have to rush back, and I'd like to see around the area as I mean to live this way.'

'We're a good twelve miles from Asterleigh Park,' Laura said, before Kate could reply.

'An easy enough distance to cover by car.' Mike was looking at Kate, who was shaking her head to his query about accompanying her on her round.

'Doctors don't usually take a passenger when they're off tending the sick.' She tried to make light of turning him down. 'I mean, what would people think?'

'I'd be in the car, practically invisible,' he pressed.

'But you're not the invisible kind.' It was true—his elegant fairness was, in its way, as eye-catching as Guy's tall, dark burliness. Well, almost. Anyway, it would be good to have him with her. She knew that this weekend he was off to Hampshire to see his parents so it would be days before she saw him again. Anyway, what harm would it do? 'Well, all right, you're on,' she agreed, refusing to look at her mother who was crashing the lunch dishes into the sink.

Mike moved his car into the garage, and they set off in the Volvo, driving through the November mist which was very nearly rain. Kate's first call was on a seventy-year-old woman who lived alone. She had rung the surgery that morning, complaining of feeling feverish and sick. Not having attended her before, Kate took a quick glance at her medical notes before she got out of the car.

As it happened, Kate hardly needed to examine her. The patient's illness was plain to see and easy to diagnose—Mrs Beresford had mumps. The glands in front of her ears were swollen, it hurt her to open her mouth, she was febrile and feeling very unwell.

'I thought it must be that,' she said, when Kate broke the news to her, 'but mumps at my age, Doctor. It's too ridiculous!'

'It's very bad luck,' Kate said as she wrote out a prescription for acetylsalicylic acid, which would help relieve her symptoms, 'but it's not unknown in older people if they escaped it in childhood. Now, you'll have to isolate yourself for a fortnight. Have you a kind neighbour who'll shop for you and get your prescription made up?'

'Yes, I have, and she's got a key so she can leave it in my kitchen, without me breathing on her.' Mrs Beresford laughed, then immediately winced, her eyes watering with pain. 'How long will I be like this?'

'I'm afraid the swelling will worsen before it gets better,' Kate warned. 'For the first few days I should rest all you can, preferably in bed. You'll need to liquidise your food and take it through a straw till you can open your mouth without pain. It's a nasty thing to have, but it's in no way serious. I'll call again next week but, in the meantime, if you're at all worried about yourself, ring the surgery.'

'Where to next?' asked Mike, when Kate got back to the car.

'Into Melbridge and through it to the new housing estate,' Kate replied, smiling at him. In spite of her earlier reluctance to have him with her in the car, it was good to see him there, waiting for her, and just for a second the way she had felt with him in the old days slipped over her like a second skin. Excitement's not everything and I still have a load of affection for him, she thought.

She had three calls to make in the vicinity of the housing estate—the first on a male patient with gout who couldn't put his foot to the floor, the second on a woman recently discharged from hospital after a hysterectomy and the third on a schoolgirl with tonsillitis whose mother was aghast when Kate refused to prescribe an antibiotic.

'But she needs one...to clear it up. Dr John would have given her one!'

'No, Mrs Turner, he wouldn't,' Kate said firmly. 'An antibiotic is only necessary in cases of severe attacks, where the glands are grossly enlarged or when there are complications. Keep Jane in bed for a few days, and give her one and a half tablets of soluble aspirin twice a day till her fever subsides. I'll call in again on Tuesday when I'm sure she'll be feeling a whole lot better.'

Kate was seen off rather curtly by Mrs Turner, who still looked unconvinced, but occasionally patients, or the relatives of patients, *did* think they knew best. It was all part of the GP's day and job, Kate thought, climbing back into the car with Mike, who took her medical case from her and laid it on the back seat. She was being looked after, and it was a pleasant feeling. 'All done now,' she said, fastening her seat belt and switching on her lights.

At that moment she caught sight of Guy, who was coming out from a house four doors down where one of her uncle's patients, a terminal case, lived with her widowed sister. He saw them—the car, her, and, of course, Mike. He flapped a hand in acknowledgment, then drove off at speed, leaving Kate wisl..ng they hadn't run into him. Not that it mattered, of course, but she still wished he hadn't seen them.

An interpretation of socialising while she was on duty would be put on the fact that Mike was with her for that was what it looked like—what it *was*, she admitted privately. Kate sighed as she pulled on her gloves, and told Mike that she'd run him back to Riverstone to get his car. 'Then you can be off to the wilds of Hampshire,' she jested, and tried to relax.

'I wish you were coming with me. My parents would love to see you again.'

'Would they?'

'Yes, of course they would.' He put his hand on her knee.

'I'm on call, I told you.'

'I know…sorry.' He removed his hand, clasping it in his lap as though keeping it there by force.

They didn't speak much as they drove back into the town centre. Kate knew he was coming down to Melbridge next week to look for living accommodation. As he was due to start at the Redlands Clinic in two weeks' time he ought to be taking positive steps. 'The best thing you can do,' she suggested, as they slid into the high street, 'is to apply to Perry's, the estate agents— that is, if you're really set on living in Melbridge.'

'I am.'

'Well, they're your best bet. They deal in furnished lets as well as unfurnished. They would find you something, even if it was only temporary. Look, those are the offices—there on your right, next to the public library. I know a bit about them because…' Kate manoeuvred carefully round a bus '…I'm in the throes of buying a house. I should get possession early next month.'

'To live in?' She had all Mike's attention.

'That's the general idea!'

'On your own?'

'Yes, I'm buying it with some of the legacy Dad left me. I never intended living at home for ever, only just till Mum found her feet.'

Mike was quiet—in fact, speechless—which meant, Kate knew, that he was too surprised to find appropriate words. He used to react like that in the days when they were living together and she'd done something, or was planning something, that he thought was over the top. Mike had never been very adventurous, had he? Look how quickly he'd come back to the UK once Caroline had loosened her grip. 'So, I should go to Perry's,' she emphasised when, after a near-silent journey, they stopped outside Riverstone and went over to the garage to get his car.

As she unlocked the door and pushed it up to roof level, he drew her under its shelter, holding her by the arm, as though he thought she might escape him before he'd had his say. 'Kate,' he began, 'I want us to buy a house together. I want us to *be* together. I want you to marry me! It's why I'm here, it's why I'm back—it's the reason for everything!'

'*Mike*!' Now, this she hadn't expected. Living together—yes, she'd thought he'd ask that eventually, but marriage was something else. Because he'd surprised her, even shocked her, all she could say was, 'I don't know. It's a big commitment.'

'But we talked about it before…before I…'

'Before you went off? Yes, I know we did, but that was then and this is now. I don't feel the same way about you.' Only honesty would do, she thought, and even in that fraught moment the imminence of evening surgery took precedence. 'We can't talk about this now, Mike. I have to go.'

'Give me a chance to make up for what I did. Don't discard me to pay me back.'

'I wouldn't do that.'

'Then give me a chance, however long it takes.' He bent to kiss her and she let it happen, but when the firm, gentle pressure deepened to something more she stepped back, releasing herself.

'Mike, I have to go. I've got to get to the surgery, and you've a long journey to make.' The musty, petrolly smell in the garage was making her head ache.

'Meet me next week when I'm down here. I'll probably stay at The Bridge.' He was making no move to detain her now.

'Yes, of course we can meet,' Kate said, running down the path to her car and turning by the hedge to wave.

She drove off in turmoil, feeling that she'd mishandled the situation—feeling that she hadn't been very kind either, all but pushing him off. He had paid her the ultimate in compliments, and she knew it. She also knew that marriage was what she wanted, and not so very long ago she had wanted it with Mike. Could she really have changed all that much?

An image of Guy swam into her mind—Guy, who would show her a glimpse of heaven but only for a time. To love him—and she was near to it—would be dangerous, folly.

Step back before it's too late, she told herself. Think about Mike and what it would mean to settle down with him. 'I can't marry a man for whom I only feel affection,' she muttered in protest. Yet plenty of people did and their marriages often worked out. Some people said that a marriage based on friendship was the best way to stay the course...

CHAPTER EIGHT

KATE was surprised to see Guy in her room when she got to Larchwood. She was the one on duty, not he. He didn't smile when she greeted him. 'Cut it a bit fine, didn't you?' He looked at his watch. 'I thought I was going to have to step in.'

'No chance,' she said, and her voice was light because she thought at first he was joking. When she saw by the set of his mouth that he wasn't she made a quiet point of telling him that there was still a clear fifteen minutes to go.

'Plenty of time for a cuppa, Dr Kate.' Enid Ford put two steaming cups on the corner of the desk.

'Mine's no doubt waiting for me through in the house so now that you're here,' Guy said as he passed Kate, 'I'll have it in peace.'

'Oh, drink this one here now you've got it.' Sylvia appeared, svelte and high-heeled in the doorway, her make-up immaculate. Her eyes went to Kate. 'I see you've got Mike back, Kate. I spotted him in your car just now when you stopped at the traffic lights. I suppose he had a sort of gap year in the States. It seems almost a cult these days, but I guess you're thrilled to have him back...'

'Well, yes, of course I am—'

'And, of course, I did *know* he was back—Guy told me that. I'm sure you must have missed him. When you used to bring him here, soon after John and I were married, you two were like cooing doves.'

'Oh, for heaven's sake, Ma.' Guy tried to shut her up.

She disregarded him and prattled on. 'And he's got a job this way. Your mother thinks you'll end up living together in your new house.'

'I'm only just getting used to Mike being back,' Kate said, burningly aware of Guy who was making restless movements. He had been on the point of leaving when his mother had burst in.

'When do you get possession of the house?' Sylvia wasn't for turning.

'On the seventh of December.' Kate wished she'd go, but she couldn't quite bring herself to look at her watch as Guy had done.

'In another couple of weeks…not long then, is it? You must bring Mike to see us.' Then she did depart, as quickly as she'd come.

Kate was sure Guy would go with her, but he closed the door after her and walked past the desk to the window where he stood, looking out.

'You mustn't take too much notice of Ma. She's just ferreting around,' he said, turning and leaning against the window-sill.

'I was actually surprised she recognised Mike. It's over three years since she's seen him.'

Guy made no comment. Instead, he said, 'Don't you think it smacks of frivolity, taking him with you on your calls? What are patients and relatives of patients likely to think when they're showing you out and see your boyfriend, waiting in the car?'

'They'll be wild with jealousy!' Kate sipped her tea, refusing to look at him.

'What they'll think,' he persisted, 'is that you're out on a spree, first and foremost, and that you've just dropped in to see them when you happened to be passing by!'

'That's *ridiculous*!' Kate put her cup down for safety

because her hand had gone nerveless. How *dared* he tell her off!

'It's true and you know it!'

'What I *know* is how to conduct myself professionally. I don't need advice on that!'

'I'm not advising so much as telling you straight...' he came forward to the desk '...that it gives a wrong impression to take your boyfriend out on calls!'

Guy was right and she knew it, but his attitude and tone made her argue the point. She looked up at him angrily, which was a fair way to cover as she was still sitting down. 'You're carping, Guy, fault-finding, being bloody-minded! You're too fond of telling people what to do and how to conduct themselves. You should have been a schoolmaster instead of a doctor—it would have given your instincts full rein!'

He didn't look wounded, she noticed. His mouth tightened a little, perhaps, and he was glinty-eyed, but otherwise seemed unaffected by her barbs. He was standing very straight, too, and moving towards the door. 'I think we had better end this conversation right now,' he said, very distinctly and distantly, just as Janice came in to tell Kate that her four-thirty patients were in the waiting-room.

Guy went out, with nothing more being said, but even when he'd gone the room seemed to rattle with angry exchanges. Kate found herself covering her ears. I won't let him upset me, she seethed. She pressed her buzzer and schooled her face, managing to smile at the mother and child who came in.

They were Mrs Stanhope and the little girl, Nell—the firework casualty whose grandfather had died on that same night of 5 November.

'How can I help you?' The notes on Kate's desk bore Nell's name. 'So, you're the patient tonight, are you?'

She looked over at the child, who nodded mutely and smiled back, loosening the scarf round her neck.

'She's lost her voice,' Ann Stanhope explained. 'She can't even speak in a whisper. It went two days after her grandfather died. She went to bed all right, or so I thought, but she woke up voiceless. I thought it was probably some sort of cold. I've kept her away from school, but now I don't know... Tom and I are worried... He said we should come to see you.'

'It's always best to get these things checked out.' Kate turned to Nell who was looking a little self-conscious and sat, nursing her bandaged hand. 'We'll have to communicate by nods and shakes, Nell. Tell me about your hand first. Is it less painful, getting better?' The child nodded and half smiled. 'So, what about your throat. Does it feel at all sore?'

Nell mouthed, 'No.'

'Well, I'd like to have a little look at it.' Reaching back, Kate took a wooden spatula from the clinical trolley, together with a pencil torch. 'Now, open your mouth as wide as you can for me, Nell, and tilt your head back...right back. That's good, that's brilliant. I know you can't speak, but make the same movement as if you were saying "ah-h-h".'

There was nothing to see, nothing untoward, nothing sinister—no white or inflamed patches, no nodules or lumps. 'OK, close up.' Kate switched off the torch and flung the spatula into the bin, choosing her next words as carefully as she could.

'There's nothing visibly wrong.' She addressed both child and parent. 'I think Nell is suffering from shock—the shock of firework night and losing her grandfather, which was dreadful for you all.'

'But...when will her voice come back?' Ann's thin face whitened.

'It's difficult to say. It could be just days, but shock can be unpredictable. I think you should see a throat specialist, Nell. We call him an ENT man. I'll send off for an appointment,' she told the girl's mother. 'Hopefully, in a few days you'll get a letter from the hospital, telling you when to go. It's likely to be a Mr Trenchard. You'll like him—most of his patients are children.'

Ann looked even more worried. 'Ought I to keep her away from school?'

Kate considered this. 'No, I don't think so,' she said. 'Just write a note to the school, explaining Nell's difficulty, and let her carry on as before. The more normally and ordinarily she's treated the better. She doesn't have to speak to learn. The very fact that she's back in the classroom with her friends might hurry things along.'

They got up. 'Well, thank you.' Ann looked down anxiously at her child, who was winding the navy-and-white school muffler round her neck again.

'Bye, then, Nell.' Kate smiled at them both, and out they went, closely followed by a heart patient who wanted a repeat prescription. It was a busy evening and long gone half past six before surgery was finished. Even so, Kate decided to write the referral letter to Mr Trenchard. She could make a slight detour and drop it in at the hospital on her way home. She was halfway through it when Guy appeared, looming large in the doorway as he bent forward with one hand on the knob.

'If I had a hat I'd throw it in!' He was half smiling, half serious.

Ignoring the little flutter in her chest and holding her pen tightly, Kate managed to say, 'Now, what exactly is that supposed to mean?'

'Men do it when they're trying to make peace with their wives after they've had a night out on the tiles.'

Kate laughed, as he'd intended she should. 'Well, that hardly applies...'

'To us, no, course not. Even so, I'd like to be forgiven for my churlish attitude earlier on.' He advanced further into the room and stood in front of her desk. Keeping her eyes determinedly level, she could see the top of his legs, his flat abdomen and one of his hands which was going into his pocket.

'Yes, you did go on a bit,' she said, 'but you were right in what you said. It would have been better to have said no to Mike and left him to get back to Fulham. Actually, I did say no at first, but then I just gave in.'

'Do you usually?'

'Usually what?' She raised startled eyes to his face.

'Give in to him?' His eyes were narrowed.

'Certainly not,' she replied, with such emphasis that he wondered if she might be protesting just a little too much—except, of course, that it wasn't his business.

Looking down at the form on her desk, he changed the subject by asking, 'Why are you writing that referral tonight? Can't it wait till tomorrow?'

'I dare say it could, but I want to drop it in at hospital on my way home,' Kate replied, wondering if he was about to tell her what to do again. Just in case he was, she went on to explain about Nell Stanhope.

'Sounds like hysterical mutism.' Guy rubbed the point of his chin. 'The trouble with these reactions is that you never know how long they'll last. I had a case of hysterical blindness once when I was practising in Cumbria. It was a young girl who'd seen her father killed on a level crossing. She remained blind for two years and had to learn to read Braille and live as an unsighted person. When her sight returned it happened suddenly one evening when the family was watching television. The first thing she saw was a commercial for stock cubes—the whole family went wild.'

'I can imagine.' Kate looked back at her letter.

'I'd better let you get on.'

'Yes, please,' she said lightly.

'But before I do…' He made his way around the desk, turned her face to his and said, inches from her mouth, 'I'm glad you don't *usually* give in to your boyfriend.' He was teasing in more ways than one. She wanted him to kiss her, but all she got was a chaste peck on the cheek. Even so, she laughed. She couldn't help it—the shared moment was worth having. 'Don't forget to lock up when you leave,' he said, turning at the door. He was being bossy again, infuriating again—in other words, true to form.

Still, Kate thought ten minutes later when she was on her way to the hospital, he'd been generous enough to apologise for barracking her earlier on. Few men would have done that—especially when they'd been in the right, as he'd been. There was nothing, she realised, mean about Guy. His nature matched his build. He was a lovely man—a lovable man—and at that point she reined in her thoughts.

The following Wednesday saw Guy, Kate, John Burnett and Sue Avers in the dining-room of The Bridge Hotel, having lunch. True to form, Sue had taken the invitation in her stride. It wasn't in her nature to be overwhelmed. She'd simply accepted with surprise and obvious pleasure.

Sue had no clinic that afternoon or evening, which was why they had chosen Wednesday. It was Kate's half-day too. In fact, the only one of them who couldn't drink wine with their meal was Guy, in deference to his afternoon visits. Conversation was relaxed, with Sue talking about her children at first.

'They're missing Clive. I've told them all the usual business of him being in heaven, but they refuse to believe he can't visit them from there. He was away so often, you see. In time they'll realise he's never coming back, but I can't keep telling them so.'

She looked mainly at Guy as she said all this, seeming to seek his approval, but by the time she was on her third glass of wine—carefully selected by Dr John—she opened up to an embarrassing degree, telling them that her husband had taken out a substantial policy on his life. 'What it means is that I and the girls will never be in want even if I decide to give up work, which I don't mean to do.'

'I'm glad for you, Susan. Not to have money worries means a very great deal.' Dr John chased a morsel of apple in filo pastry around the rim of his plate. 'But I'm relieved to hear you say that you don't mean to give us the sack!'

'Once a nurse always a nurse—at least, so they say.' Sue's glance was on Guy again, who nodded and agreed with her.

'Especially,' he said, 'when the nurse takes a mountain of work off the poor old GP!'

'Not so much of the "old"!' Dr John pretended to glower at him. They all laughed, including Kate, who was a little *distraite*. Mike was due to arrive at the hotel that evening to start his search for living accommodation in the area. She wished she felt more thrilled about him coming. She would be pleased to see him, of course— in fact, she was looking forward to it. It'll be fine, just fine, she thought, looking up to meet Guy's eye and flinching away from it.

On the whole, though, it was a successful lunch. Guy

was giving each of them a lift home, before starting his calls. Dr John, however, had an appointment at the hospital for treatment to his arm in the form of intensive physiotherapy, which he declared was worse than breaking it in the first place.

They were crossing the foyer towards the doors when Kate spotted Mike, signing in at the curved reception desk. There was no mistaking that grey flannel suit or the fair head above it. Mike's build made him look taller than he actually was. As he swung round with his bag in his hand he came face to face with the four of them, his expression lightening as his eyes fell on Kate. 'It's all right, it's not a reception committee.' She laughed and touched his arm. 'We've been lunching here. You remember Uncle John?' She stepped back and the two shook hands.

'Good to see you again, Mike. Heard you were back and had a job lined up. Well done, a good physio is worth his weight in gold.' Not knowing all the circumstances of Mike's defection, he was all smiles and *bonhomie*, which masked any doubts he might have.

Kate introduced Sue. 'Mike, this is Susan Avers, our practice nurse. Sue, this is Michael Merrow, recently back from the States.'

'Now, that's somewhere I've always wanted to go to,' Sue enthused, interest plain on her face as the two of them shook hands. She asked Mike if he would be working at the General. When she was told that he'd be at the Redlands Clinic she said that a friend of hers was nursing there. 'It's seriously elite.'

Guy was making restless movements. He wanted to be off, Kate knew. Any minute now he'd be looking at his watch so she cut in and told Mike she'd see him later on. They made their way out to the car park, battling against a gusty wind which made them duck, and were glad to climb into the Rover. Sue sat in front with Guy, Kate in the back with Dr John who pointed out that young Merrow must have made a pile in America if he could afford to stay at The Bridge.

'He looks the part, though, doesn't he?' Sue craned her neck round to the back. 'He'll go down like a bomb at Redlands.' Kate knew what she meant, and agreed.

On Friday she helped Sue clear up after the Well-Woman clinic. She felt Sue was pushing herself too hard—all that frenetic energy flying around. 'Go off home, Sue,' she said. 'You've been brilliant to come in this week.'

'No reason not to. I'm all right.' She sat for a second, then jumped up, sat down again and said that she hoped she hadn't been too 'mouthy' during their lunch at The Bridge. 'Drink always gets to me,' she said, and was up again to strip the couch.

'I'm the same, and you were fine.' Kate was frowning at a form which had had something disgusting spilled on it. As she reached for another she was startled to hear Sue declare that she intended to have a good time from now on.

'I know Clive has only just died...' she folded a towel into squares '...but you must be able to see that I'm not bowed down with grief. We weren't happy together, not after the kids were born. I certainly don't mean to marry again—I'm done with all that. I shall see that the kids are all right, of course, and they'll never want for anything, but I don't see why I shouldn't have something *now*, just for myself. It'll be good to have the money— it'll make things easier. Clive did me a favour there.'

'Oh, Sue.' Kate put down her pen. She didn't know what to say.

'No need to look shocked. At least I'm honest. I mean to enjoy myself—get myself a life, as they say.'

'I don't blame you,' Kate said. She thought that Clive must have hurt Sue badly for all this to come tumbling out so soon after his death.

'You really *are* shocked, aren't you?' Sue smoothed back her cloud of dark hair.

'Rigid!' Kate smiled.

Sue looked at her curiously. 'What about you and that fair-haired Adonis just back from America?'

'What about him?'

'Well, *you* know.' Sue wasn't to be put off. 'Why did he go to America?'

'To gain experience.' That, Kate thought wryly, was one way of putting it, and Sue could make of it what she liked.

She had seen Mike every day since he'd been at The Bridge, but they had laid down one or two ground rules—or at least she had, telling him frankly that her feelings for him had changed but that she was still very fond of him.

'That'll do to start off with. We can build on that.' He'd held tightly to her hands, as though trying to instil what *he* felt into them. 'I won't pressure you in any way,' he'd promised when he'd kissed her goodnight, rubbing his face against hers. He'd asked her if there was anyone else, and she'd shaken her head, although to be truthful she'd have had to say that there was, but that he only wanted her for a fling, whereas she wanted what Mike had offered her—marriage—and that she was hoping her feelings would change.

On Wednesday he was offered a furnished flat by the inimitable Mr Perry, who had contacts at Asterleigh Park. It was a mere half-mile from Redlands Clinic, and was available while its owner was visiting relatives in Japan. 'It's only for three months,' Mike told Kate, 'but it'll do for the time being.'

Kate helped him move in during the weekend before he was due to start at Redlands—not that there was much to move for the flat had every mod con. It was just a case of filling the fridge and freezer while Mike unpacked his clothes.

They talked companionably together as they worked, calling out to one another from bedroom to kitchen and back again. It reminded Kate of so much. Nostalgia was uncomfortable—it was also a deceiver because it led one to think that feelings hadn't changed all that much and could be beckoned back again.

Grantford church clock was striking four as she made the turn into Guessens Road. Mike and she were going to the leisure centre out at Barham this evening. There was to be a gala opening of the new ice rink, and he, being a very good skater, was keen to go. He'd tried to teach Kate in the Mamesbury days, but she'd never really enjoyed it. Tonight she'd be happy to sit and watch in one of the ringside seats.

'Whose car are you going in?' Laura asked Kate over supper.

'Mine,' Kate replied. 'I'm on call so I might need it. Mike is leaving his here. We shan't be late back— around ten or half past.'

'You'll probably see Guy there,' Laura said thoughtfully, cutting herself some more cheese. 'I met him at Melbridge this afternoon with Susan Avers. They, or rather he, carried my shopping to the car.'

'Guy and Sue! What were they doing?' Kate's voice rose.

'Shopping, I suppose. Guy had bought a pair of skating boots from that sports shop in Middle Street. Susan had been advising him, so she said. It was then that they told me they were going skating tonight.'

'*Together*?' Kate was still incredulous.

'Apparently, yes. Kate, Guy needs to relax, you know, and someone to relax *with*. Susan's an attractive young woman and, before you say that her husband has only just died, I should imagine she needs to get out and have a little fun. What's she supposed to do—sit at home and mope with a cloth over her head?'

'She told me last week that she intended to get herself a life.'

'Well, then, that's what she's doing, and that, I think...' she turned her head towards the curtained window '...sounds like Mike's car.'

He came in, swinging his boots by the laces. He looked eager and young, a black leather jacket over his jeans, his fair hair slicked from his brow. 'I haven't skated for two years,' he said, as he got into the car.

'Oh, you didn't do it in Boston, then?' Kate asked as she pulled off.

'No,' he said shortly. 'Let's forget about that, shall we, and concentrate on now? I'm home, and I'm settled, and hopeful.' He took her hand and kissed its back. 'Darling, Kate, I love you, and I feel anything's possible!'

She didn't reply—she couldn't—but, then, she was driving the car, which took all her attention as the traffic was heavy all the way out to Barham Rise. They went straight to the rink and to the seats at the side, where Mike put on his boots then made his way to the ice, where he glided off like a pro. He looked graceful and confident, his arms scarcely moving, his balance perfect.

The rink was fairly crowded and becoming more so for this was a special night, but no one seemed to clash with anyone else and there was a friendly atmosphere. Mike, for sheer grace, and prowess and skill, stood out from the rest. Several spectators were pointing at him, and Kate felt proud as she heard their comments, saving them up to tell him later on. She watched him for minutes only, however, as amongst the weaving figures she saw Guy and Sue, skating as a pair, their hands linked and looking intent. They didn't see her as they glided past then merged with the crowd again.

Suddenly, Mike was coming over to sit with her again. He was excited. 'It's brilliant, Kate! Oh, I wish you could partner me!'

'Well, I can't, can I? I'm a hick on skates, as you know very well!'

Guy and Sue were just about to pass again, and as her eyes followed them she heard Mike say, 'That's your cousin, isn't it, and that pert little nurse? As a pair they hardly match, do they? He's too big for her. He baulks her glides, and she foreshortens his. Even so, they're both good, she especially.'

Kate didn't want to watch them, yet couldn't help doing so. They were laughing together now and having fun, and she was jealous and knew it—not jealous of the fun but jealous of Sue, having it with Guy. But I must smile and lump it, she thought. They've seen us and they're coming over.

Greetings were effusive, if a little forced. 'We knew you'd be here,' Guy said. 'We met your mother in the town and she mentioned it.'

'We were buying gear.' Sue sat with her weighted feet stretched out in front. Guy, in cords and one of his sweaters, was pulling the high roll collar away from his neck.

'Sue's worn me out. I'm not in her league!'

'You're good, though, or would be with practice.' Sue tied her hair back from her face. She was in black leggings and a ribbed scarlet jersey. She looked at Mike.

'Are you having a go? And what about you, Kate?' Her gaze dropped to Kate's white trainers.

'Not me, but I know Mike is dying to partner you.'

'Well, yes.' Mike coloured. 'It's more fun to pair-skate than go around on one's own.'

Off they went, and Guy and Kate watched them. They were soon excelling themselves, performing turns and twirls, jumps and glides, evoking applause.

'Don't you skate at all?' Guy asked her.

'Oh, yes, after a fashion. Mike taught me years ago, but I never really took to it. Swimming and squash are my favourite sports.'

'Squash is a very fast game.'

'That's true, but your feet are your own.'

'That reminds me...' He bent and took the skates off his boots. As he straightened he turned and looked at Kate. She could feel him doing so as acutely as though his look were a touch—a burn against her skin.

'We've been having a busy time lately, haven't we—within the practice, I mean?' she said quickly and confusedly, her eyes on the skaters, not daring to look at him.

'We both deserve our leisure.'

'Yes.' There was a lump in Kate's throat like a rock. If only they could share it together. Oh, how could he turn to Sue? Was it for consolation, and was she finding it with him? Her mind flicked away from the possibility that they were already lovers. Sue's marriage had been unhappy. She'd been a neglected wife, and that usually meant—

'Sue's great company,' Guy remarked in that spooky and maddening way he had of tuning in to her thoughts.

'I'm sure she is. She deserves a good time,' Kate said, slewing her eyes sideways to him without moving her head. His chair was slightly higher than hers, and she could see his hand, sticking out from the sleeve of his sweater, as it lay on the wooden arm. Her thoughts focussed on nothing else, certainly not on Sue who had purloined Mike and was very nearly putting him through hoops on ice. Guy's hand was so still it was very nearly admonitory, and she felt told off, without a single word being said.

'I think our partners are about to rejoin us,' he commented, getting to his feet as Sue put a skinny leg over the rail, closely followed by Mike.

'Now that was truly sensational,' Sue enthused as they bent to remove their skates. 'You can lend him to me another evening.' The remark had been intended for Kate, but was taken up by Mike who good-humouredly said he wasn't a bestseller book but that if he were he'd be Kate's for all time and not for lending out.

At Sue's suggestion—it was very much Sue's evening—they went along to the restaurant, where they drank hot chocolate and ate torpedo rolls filled with ham and cheese. Guy was eating with relish. It was he who mentioned the Christmas Dance which was to be held at the Melbridge Assembly Rooms a week that night.

'There were posters all over the town this morning. It's in aid of the Red Cross. Will you two be going?' He looked over at Kate and Mike, who nodded, then went on to praise the work the society did for Third World countries. This led to Mike asking him about Mtanga, and pretty soon they were deep in conversation about conditions in Africa.

Surely, Kate thought, watching them carefully, they shouldn't be getting on so well. If Guy thinks anything about me at all he should be sniffy with Mike, a shade antagonistic. Any minute now he'll be suggesting we go to that dance in a foursome.

She was right. He did. Mike was all for it and so was

Sue. Outnumbered, Kate forced her mouth into a smile and said what fun it would be.

As she drove home with Mike beside her, he rubbed his calves and said how out of practice he was. 'I've not skated for over two years. Susan Avers is a natural, of course.'

'Yes, I noticed that.'

'Are she and Guy an item?'

'I don't know.' Kate's insides clenched. 'If they are,' she went on, 'she's a fast worker as well as a skater. Her husband has only been dead three weeks…three weeks tonight.' Her voice petered out as she brought her attention back to the road.

'I wished it had been you I was skating with,' Mike hastened to say, perhaps misinterpreting her silence. 'I hated it, not being you.'

'Oh, for heaven's sake, Mike, you don't have to console me,' she flashed. 'I wasn't jealous, if that's what you mean. I was glad you were enjoying yourself.'

'I like to keep the record straight, that's all,' he said quietly in a hurt voice.

She felt mean and uncomfortable then. He was so wide of the mark. Seeing him and Sue together hadn't caused her so much as a pang, whereas seeing her with Guy was like being stabbed. Oh, how *could* he suggest they went out in a foursome? What a gruesome thought! What was he trying to do—rub her nose in the fact that he'd found consolation in Sue? Why, only three weeks ago he'd been suggesting that *we* should be an item, she thought in a series of hops just as Mike remarked on how much he was looking forward to the dance. 'It'll be a fitting end to my first week at Redlands. First times and first weeks are the pits so I'll be thankful when Saturday comes.'

'Redlands is lucky to get you,' Kate assured him, slipping naturally back into her role of morale-booster. Mike needed encouragement. What they had...what they *still* had mattered. Excitement wasn't everything.

She felt a measure of calm, even rightness, which sustained her for the time it took to turn into Guessens Road and down it to Riverstone's white-painted gates. But there it left her, draining off in a bolting rush of alarm as her headlamps picked out a police car in the drive.

[faint text from previous page bleeding through, illegible]

CHAPTER NINE

KATE'S first thought was that something had happened to her mother. All but falling out of the car, she rushed to the front door, which opened as she reached it, and she found herself face to face with two uniformed officers. 'What's happened...? Why are you here?' She all but shouted the words then, seeing her mother coming out of the sitting-room, she pushed past the policemen and took Laura's arm. 'Oh, Mum, thank goodness... thank goodness. I thought...'

'Someone's broken in. We've been burgled.' Laura was shaking and ashen-faced.

'So long as you're OK nothing else matters.' Kate took her back into the sitting-room, only dimly aware of the police and Mike having a discussion in the hall. The sitting-room looked different with the mantelshelf bare.

'They took the clock and the ornaments and that silver-framed photograph of your father and me and no end of things upstairs, Kate, and money from the kitchen drawer. I didn't realise... I didn't know anything had happened at first. I had supper with the Pattinsons, as you know. When I got in I went straight through to the loo and there I found the window bashed in. That's how they got in—there was glass all over the place. So I rang the police and they've been all over the house. They were just going when you came in.'

'God, how awful...how awful!' Kate kept her arm around her mother. In the hall she could hear one of the policemen speaking on his mobile, although she couldn't distinguish the words. Why were they still talking to

Mike? He knew nothing about the house or what might have been taken. What was going on? The police were going now and called back to her mother, saying they'd be in touch. It was then that Mike came into the sitting-room, looking nearly as white and upset as her mother.

'Mike?' Kate rose to her feet.

'My car's gone...been taken... Used as a get-away vehicle!'

Was there no end to this nightmare? 'Oh, Mike, I'm so sorry!' Kate cried.

'I've given the police details and their patrol cars will be on the lookout for it—hopefully with the thief, or thieves, still inside it but more likely abandoned some-where, probably in a ditch.' Mike sank rather than sat on the couch beside Laura, who put a comforting hand on his arm. He asked her if much had been taken, and Kate left them talking while she rang Dr John. She was sure he would come. Her mother needed his support.

He was horrified and was at Riverstone in less than twenty minutes. Sylvia was with him, and Guy, too. Even at that fraught time Kate could still feel relieved that he wasn't spending the night with Sue. He and Mike went out to the shed and found slats of wood to nail across the window-frame of the loo, making a terrible din.

Sylvia, left with Kate, Laura and Dr John, couldn't refrain from pointing out that it had been a disaster, wait-ing to happen. 'I mean, darlings, a house of this size with only you two in it, and with both of you out so often... What can you expect? You ought to live further into the town in a much smaller place...or let part of this.'

'I don't think,' Guy said, returning with Mike, 'that Laura wants to be preached at tonight, Ma.'

Sylvia shrugged and turned to Mike. 'And I'm so

sorry about your car...such bad luck! How will you manage next week, getting to and from your job?'

'I can manage the walk. My flat's near the clinic.' He wasn't making a fuss, Kate saw, and was filled with gratitude. Mike had many good points. Even so, she was a little surprised when her mother asked him to stay the night. Perhaps, as his car had been stolen from their driveway, she'd felt it had been really the least she could do. He agreed at once and Sylvia applauded.

'A man in the house at a time like this means a hell of a lot,' she said, as they went upstairs to deal with the chaos there. And chaotic it was, with drawers pulled out and emptied onto the floor, clothes cupboard doors swinging wide and mattresses pulled off the beds.

'Perhaps they hoped to find a gold bullion room or a duvet of precious stones,' Laura said feebly, trying to joke. 'As it is, they've taken everything that's precious to me and to Kate.'

'Well, let's get cleared up,' Sylvia said practically, and turned to with a will. She was by no means all froth and bubble in a crisis, just a mite tactless.

Once downstairs again, they seemed to fall into three separate pairs—Sylvia with Mike, Dr John with Laura, Kate with Guy. They drank strong coffee with sugar in it for shock. Kate pulled a wry face at hers. Afterwards Guy carried the tray out for her. 'What a thing to come home to,' he said, and watched her rinse the cups under the hot tap, sending up billows of steam.

Kate nodded. 'But worse, though, for Mum,' she said, 'coming in all on her own. It's lucky she didn't disturb the thieves or she might have been hurt.' Her voice sounded odd—the events of the evening were beginning to get to her.

Guy was standing between her and the door, and as she made to stumble past him he wrapped his arms around her, held her against him and murmured into her hair. It was bliss, it was heaven, it was comfort and warmth, it was much, much more. Oh, if only it was he who was staying the night and not Mike. She returned his hug then quickly freed herself as she heard the others, coming out into the hall.

Minutes later they were all driving off, and she was taking Mike upstairs to find him a toothbrush and show him into the spare room. They said goodnight on the landing—an embarrassed, awkward goodnight. Each of them, even after all that had happened, was painfully aware that the last time Mike had slept at Riverstone the spare room hadn't been used.

After Kate had driven him to Asterleigh next morning her mother and she went over to Larchwood to lunch, but Guy wasn't there. 'He's at Grantford, having lunch with the Graingers,' Sylvia said. 'You probably passed him on the way.'

'Maybe we did,' Kate replied, trying not to show the mixture of disappointment and relief that was washing over her.

Conversation over the perfectly cooked roast beef was mainly about the break-in, but at least Sylvia refrained—probably warned off by Dr John—from mentioning the advisability of moving house or converting Riverstone. It was plain, though, that houses were still on her mind because she asked Kate about hers.

'Contracts are due to be exchanged on Wednesday, completion's on Friday and I move in on Saturday,' Kate said happily. 'When I say "move in" I mean I get possession. I shan't actually live in it yet.'

'She's bought it with several items of furniture so she *could* move,' Laura put in, 'but she won't because of last night. I keep telling her that lightning never strikes in the same place twice.'

'Sometimes it does,' Sylvia said darkly, but wisely left it at that while Kate hurried to say that she'd got her move scheduled for some time after Christmas.

As she spoke her glance strayed to the view of the garden beyond the big bay window, noting the frost on the grass. Winter was here with a vengeance. There had been black ice on the secondary roads earlier on when she'd driven Mike back to Asterleigh. Part of the lake had been frozen and one or two displaced ducks had been crouched on the bank, looking anxious as their companions braved the ice.

Mike had looked a forlorn figure as he and Kate had waited in the entrance hall of the flats for the lift to descend. He was due to start his new job next day, and it really was too bad, Kate had thought, that he should have been involved in their break-in and lost his car as well. The lift had arrived at last, and they'd parted in the foyer with a swift kiss, which even he hadn't seemed to want to prolong.

'I think I'll ring up and see how Mike is,' she said to Laura that evening, but no sooner had the words left her lips than the telephone rang in the hall. It was Mike, ringing to say that the police had found his car.

'It was on the other side of Challoners Lock, out on the Pentney Hook Road. It was stripped, of course—the radio, CD player, even the spare tyre in the boot. The thief, or thieves, must have had a van waiting—the police think it was carefully planned. They've towed my car in. It'll be days, I expect, before I get it back and then it'll need to be refitted, but, still, thank God, it's safe!' She was glad for him, and said so.

'You've been great about it, Mike, and thanks again for staying last night.'

'Pity it had to be in those circumstances,' he said after a pause, weighting his words with a double meaning, which Kate couldn't fail to comprehend. She decided to ignore it, telling him that she and her mother were compiling a list of everything that had been taken and that she must go and get on with it.

'I'm sure we'll leave something out—we're bound to,' Laura said with a sigh as Kate rejoined her in the sitting-room. 'And we need two lists—one for the police and one for the insurance company.'

'Oh, I'll type it out in the office at the surgery tomorrow,' Kate said. 'I'll go in early before anyone's about.'

'I feel we've been stripped and violated. The house itself has changed.' Laura shuddered, closing her eyes, but although Kate could sympathise she was glad her own reaction to the break-in was one of anger and didn't affect her love of the house.

Seven forty-five next morning found Kate in the office at Larchwood, sitting in front of the typewriter. Lack of typewriting experience made her slow. She needed to concentrate so she failed to hear the link passage door open till a large shadow fell on the counter. She looked up to see Guy leaning over it, trying to see what she was about. He came round to stand behind her chair, getting a closer look.

'I thought it was a little early for the staff to be here,' he said. He smelled of early morning—soap, toothpaste and aftershave, and just a little of toast.

'I'm typing the lists for the police and insurance company, but I expect we've left something out. It's not so easy to discover exactly what's missing, down to the last thing.' His nearness was making her tremble, which in turn made her furious. How could she possibly keep on typing when he was breathing down her neck? 'I won't be long,' she added pointedly, pushing down the correction key to change 'hold' to 'gold' and 'hooch' to brooch' and wishing he'd back off.

He moved from behind her but stayed in the office, perched on one of the stools. 'How's Laura this morning?' he ventured after a pause.

'Still shattered, but trying to come to terms with it all. The police, by the way, have found Mike's car out at Pentney, five miles away. It's damaged, but not too badly. He won't have it back for some days. He rang me last night. He's pleased, of course.' Kate put another sheet of A4 paper in the machine, willing her hands not to shake.

To the news about Mike's car, Guy muttered, 'Good.' Then he astonished her by offering to type the rest of the list. 'I'm not bad on the keys, and if you call the items out we can get the job done in no time.'

Hiding her surprise, Kate kept her voice as light as his. 'Sounds like an offer not to be missed. I didn't know you could type!'

'I'm full of surprises!' He took her seat and she stood at his shoulder. She tried to concentrate on the list and to keep her eyes from straying to the back of his head, where the dark, crisp, brushed-flat hair tapered to the rim of his collar. She spotted grey hairs and tenderness flooded her, as did the passionate desire to stoop and lay her cheek alongside his, and against his ear, and to whisper into it... What would he say if she did?

'Not come to a grinding halt already?' His voice made her jump.

'Sorry, lost my place.' She went off at a gallop and he had to ask her to stop. Even so, the list was completed and in her hands a few minutes later. 'It's fantastic...' Nervousness made her lavish with her thanks.

'Glad to help. Let me know if—' He broke off as the

street door opened to admit Meg and Janice, with Sue
bringing up the rear.

Briefly Kate told them about the burglary, but there
was no time to chat as the two patients booked in for
eight-thirty were already entering, with a dozen others
for repeat prescriptions and three for Sue's ministrations.
Kate and Guy went into their rooms. Monday surgery
had begun.

The fifteen-year-old girl whom Kate saw first was
covered in blotches—literally from head to toe, as Kate
saw when she undressed. Even as she examined her
more blotches appeared, and the girl wriggled as she sat.
'The irritation is driving me mad. I can't go to school
like this.'

'No, I don't think you can.' Kate looked carefully at
the raised pink papules, especially those on her face.
'How long have you been like this, Marian?'

'Only since this morning. I got out of bed, and then
they started to come. As I cycled over here just now I
could feel them pricking and burning on my face.
Whatever can it be?'

'It's urticaria, a form of nettle-rash—in other words,
an allergy. You're allergic to something you've been eating or drinking. Have you ever had it before?'

'No, never.'

'Then have you been eating anything unusual over the
weekend? Think back over yesterday, starting with
breakfast. You can get dressed now.'

'Nothing for breakfast, I slept in. We had the usual
Sunday roast at one o'clock and sandwiches for tea—
the take-away sort from the supermarket. Mum got them
the day before. They'd got prawns in them. I made a pig
of myself and my boyfriend laughed at me.'

'Prawns... Now, they could be the trigger.' Kate was
onto this at once.

'But we all had them, Doctor. I'm the only one with spots!'

'Because you're allergic to shellfish and they obviously aren't.' Kate reached for her pad. 'Now, I'm going to put you on a light dose of antihistamine. Take one tablet when you get home and another when you go to bed. I think you'll find by this time tomorrow that your spots will have disappeared as quickly as they came, but keep off shellfish—especially prawns!'

'Too right I will!' Marian, a devotee of Australian soaps, took herself off, still scratching but looking more cheerful than when she'd come in.

After an overweight man with low back pain, a young mother with insomnia, five patients with respiratory complaints and a youth with multiple boils, Ann Stanhope came into the consulting room with her still voiceless daughter. She had taken Nell to see the ENT consultant privately, and his letter to Kate lay on her blotter. She had read it earlier.

I saw your patient, Helen Stanhope, at my rooms this morning. Her larynx shows nothing of a sinister nature and, after questioning the mother, I am of opinion that her mutism is hysterical in origin. I consider that no useful purpose would be served by referring her to a counsellor or psychiatrist at this stage. Cases such as these usually recover spontaneously. I have advised Mrs Stanhope to keep Helen at school and treat her as normally as possible.

'He told me that Nell is a healthy girl, and that we've nothing to worry about.' Ann Stanhope told Kate doubtfully. 'But what we want to know is how long is she going to be like this?'

'Well, of course you do, but I'm afraid it's impossible

to say. It's simply a question of wait and see.' Kate smiled at them both, then wondered if she *should* be smiling when she couldn't do much to help.

'My husband wondered if a holiday would hurry things up. We'll soon be into the Christmas break, and if he could get time off work we could go to Spain for a week or ten days—somewhere nice and warm. Nell's keen to go...' Mum and child exchanged smiles '...but we want to do what's best.'

'I think it's a great idea, especially going as a family. I wish I could get away out of this winter chill.' Kate was speaking mainly to Nell, trying to gauge her reactions. Nell gave a nod in reply and mouthed, 'Thanks.' Then they left, the child in her navy school coat and beret, the mother in an anorak.

Surgery finished at last and the street door was closed, but the phones were busy as patients rang in to make appointments for the rest of the week or to request home visits or to ask to see the nurse.

Sue, who was clearing her treatment room, made a point of seeing Kate, catching her when she was on the point of starting out on her calls. 'I'm really sorry about the break-in, Kate. What a grim thing to happen. Your poor mother!' She returned Kate's auriscope, placing it on the desk.

'Yes, it was awful. Some of the things taken were the ones she valued most...belonging to my father, or things he'd given her.'

'It wasn't exactly a picnic for either of you.' Guy came out of his room, shrugging his jacket in place.

'That's true enough.' Kate sighed and grimaced. 'Most of my twenty-first presents went and other jewellery. Still, they left my tiara, I'm happy to say!' She was trying to cheer up and joke. 'Let's hope the thief doesn't track me to my house in Fallerton Road—not that I've much left worth taking now, apart from my car.'

'Wasn't it awful about Mike's car!' Sue was onto this at once.

'Yes, poor man, and he was so good about it. The police have got it now.'

'Will he get it back for Saturday night—I mean, for the dance?'

'I don't know.' Kate took the bundle of case notes from Meg that she'd need on her visits. As she stuffed them into her bag she was aware of Guy, holding the street door open ready for her to pass through. 'If he doesn't get it back he'll hire one, I expect, or I'll fetch him or something.' Brushing past Guy with a brief word of thanks, she made her way to her car.

'Isn't it on Saturday that you get possession of Mayfield Cottage?' he asked her when they met briefly at the surgery, before parting again for lunch. The staff had already left and they were alone in the office. Kate wanted another envelope of notes and went to the rack to get it.

'Yes, Saturday's the big day!' She thrilled at the thought. 'I'm collecting the keys first thing from Perry's, and will spend most of the day there. I'm not moving yet but I want to get everything ready—like the heating, for instance, especially now that we're getting hard frosts. It's useful that I was able to buy some of the furniture to start off with, and if Mike likes to stay there after the dance he can, with all mod cons laid on!'

Guy started to move off towards the link passage, medical case in hand. 'Mike appears,' he said, 'to be one of those men who always falls on his feet. Not only has he got his car back, but his girlfriend as well!'

'I'm not lost property, Guy, and I don't go with the

house!' Kate was angered but tried to hide it, not that Guy seemed to care.

'Catch you later!' he said breezily, going through into the house.

On Thursday Mike telephoned to say that his car was still in dock and that he wouldn't have it for Saturday's dance. 'Well, that's the bad news,' he carried on cheerfully. 'The good is that the job's going well so I seem to have made the right choice. Walking to and from the clinic every day is keeping me fit. I'm all for limbering up, as you know, and—'

'Mike, about Saturday,' Kate interrupted. 'I'll come and collect you. It'll save you hiring a car or getting a taxi, and you can use the house—my house, Mayfield—and stay there the night.'

'Why, Kate, that's—'

'I shall be at home at Riverstone...you'll be on your own.'

'Point taken, but offer accepted.' He sounded just a shade less ecstatic, she thought, but still very pleased.

Kate had a pre-employment medical examination to carry out first thing on Saturday morning, the patient being a young woman of twenty-five called Zelda Bates. She had applied for a post with a haulage company, which entailed driving heavy goods vehicles. She was tiny and wiry, looking more like a dancer than a driver of lorries and vans.

'Have you done this kind of work before?' Kate looked at the letter from Zelda's firm and the long questionnaire attached as she reached for her sphygmomanometer.

'My father was a builder.' Zelda watched the cuff, being wrapped round her upper arm. 'I used to drive his lorries to and from the sites. He's retired now—heart trouble—so I've applied for this job. I like driving—don't want to do anything else.'

'Well, your blood pressure's fine.' Kate carried on with the detailed examination—heart and lungs next, weight and height, visual acuity, urine testing. 'Any trouble with your ears?' She picked up her auriscope.

'I'm not deaf, if that's what you mean.'

'No lumbago or rheumatic pains?'

'No.' Zelda watched Kate completing the form, knowing that what was said on it would make or break her chances.

Kate could feel the anxiety wafting across the desk. 'It's all right, Miss Bates.' She smiled at the girl. 'You seem to be perfectly fit. I'll be posting this off to your company this morning.'

'Oh, thanks, great, thanks very much!' Zelda shot to her feet, grabbed her jacket and hurried out and down the drive to the kerbside, where her boyfriend waited in a car and trailer, loaded with Christmas trees.

With not long to go until Christmas, Melbridge was transformed. Three of Marrisons' plate-glass windows were given over to scenes from *A Christmas Carol*—Scrooge, Tiny Tim and all. Boots had a Santa and grinning reindeer, swooping over its soaps. Smith's had a tree festooned with lanterns in the shape of children's books. Even Mr Perry had a careful outline of fairy lights around his door, Kate noticed when she collected her keys just after eleven o'clock.

Kate felt nervous as she turned into Fallerton Road and stopped outside the house. She had visited twice while the purchase was going through, but never on her own—never as its owner—which made, she was discovering, a tremendous difference. Her stomach rumbled as she walked up the garden path.

She needn't have worried. If anything the little house looked even more welcoming this morning, with the pale winter sun on its white walls and green pantile roof. It was detached and private but not too far from its neighbours, and Kate was glad about that. Maybe, she thought, in time she *would* let part of it off, perhaps to a nurse from the hospital. Nurses were always looking for rooms.

She put the key in the lock, turned it and the door swung back. Still holding her breath, she stepped inside and was instantly reassured. Yes, it was going to be all right. The friendly atmosphere she had noticed on her previous visits was still around, was still in evidence. What had she worried about?

Her feet sank into soft carpets as she toured the ground-floor rooms, pulling back curtains to let in the sun which showed up motes of dust. She'd enjoy cleaning up—this was her house, her very own house. She exalted at the thought as she went upstairs to view the three rooms there. One of them was fully furnished— Mike's for tonight. He was bringing his own duvet. She decided, signing her name in dust on top of a chest of drawers, to clean in there first. Mike, who was fastidious, wouldn't appreciate sharing space with dust mites.

On her way out she opened the landing window, then went downstairs to get the gas boiler going and fetch her cleaning things. Lighting the boiler, however, proved to be impossible. Even when she lay in front of it, staring at its undercarriage, she couldn't locate the pilot-light jet, and after six attempts and half a box of matches she had to concede defeat. Why couldn't it be one of those modern ones you can light by pressing a button? she thought, feeling vexed as she dusted her knees. Now I can't get the heating going, damn it, and the place is like a fridge.

Sweeps of icy air were blowing down from the landing window. She went up to close it and glancing down as she fastened the catch, saw Guy—unfamiliar in a bulky overcoat—striding up the garden path. Why had he come? What did he want? Excitement bounced inside her. She was halfway down the stairs when the bell pealed, shivering the silence into fragments. She opened the door to a foot-stamping Guy, his coat collar turned up around his ears.

'Guy… Hello.' Her voice rose in query.

'May I come in? And there's nothing wrong so don't look so shocked!' He wiped his feet on the mat, closed the door with his back and took out a small box from his pocket. 'A small gift from your uncle and Ma and me to grace your little house!'

'What is it?'

'Open it, but what have we here?' he asked, as they entered the kitchen. Kate's spent matches still littered the floor where the boiler door swung wide.

'I can't light it… I can't light the boiler! I've been trying and trying, and I can't!'

'Boilers can be tricky devils!' He took off his coat, laying it along one of the work tops, then crouched on his heels. 'Why don't you open your parcel while I'm wrestling with this?'

'OK, will do.' It was a smallish box, but heavy in her hands. She lifted the lid and saw tissue paper, then— nestling in packing—a tiny ormolu bedside clock, a near replica of the one her father had given her and which had been stolen by the burglars. She lifted it out, speechless with pleasure. 'How ever did you manage to find one so like…so like my other?'

'By good luck and diligent searching! Truthfully, I didn't know that was the same, but I thought you'd like it.' He rose to his feet with a grin, indicating the now

purring boiler. 'Mission accomplished!' He brought his
hands together in a clap, pleased with himself.

'Brilliant!' Kate laughed. 'And, Guy, thank you for
the clock. I'll take it home until I move in properly and
use it at Riverstone.'

'It's from the three of us, you know.' He seemed to
want to make that clear, she thought.

'I know—you said. I'll ring Uncle John and Sylvia
tonight.'

'I'll go and check the radiators—make sure they're
heating.' He moved towards the stairs, ending a pause
rife with embarrassment, at least on Kate's side. She
knew why it was. They were alone together...with beds
and things upstairs. When he came back she was in the
sitting-room, dusting the mantelshelf. He called her
name, then came in. She could see him in the mirror as
he came up behind her, holding her gaze with his.

'Are you going now?' She turned, finding him dan-
gerously near.

'Yes, I'm aware of the proprieties, and of all the hazards as well!' His eyes teased her but his hands were
gentle as they cupped her shoulders—tentative hands,
questioning hands. In the end it was she who took the
initiative, and moved closer still, reaching on tiptoe to
pull his head down to hers.

His response was immediate. He spoke her name
once, then his mouth was over hers, moving softly from
side to side, his tongue like silk exploring the inner side
of her lip, cascading her into delight, into a torrent of
emotion so overwhelming that she almost lost conscious-
ness.

When the doorbell ripped its summons through the
house it was like being dashed to earth—back to the
world, back to reality. She heard Guy's muttered curse.

When his arms left her she wanted to protest and when he stepped back she could have cried.

'I think you ought to answer that, don't you?' he said, as the bell rang again. He sounded calm and collected, which stiffened her at once.

'I can't think who it can be,' Kate said tartly, jerking her jumper down and going to the door on legs that threatened to give way at the knees.

On the step, her face rosy and smiling under a red woollen cap, stood Sue with a fair-sized carton clutched to her front. She held it out. 'A house present from all of us—the staff at Larchwood—with our love and best wishes, and for God's sake don't drop it—you're holding a load of glass!'

'Oh, Sue, how kind.' Kate managed to smile. 'Come in for a minute,' she said, fairly unnecessarily, for Sue was already in. She looked about her, her eyes widening when Guy emerged from the sitting-room.

'Why, Doctor!' she sketched a bow.

'Hello, Sue, what brings you here?' His smile was easy and appreciative. 'I like the titfer,' he said.

She laughed and dragged it off, shaking her dark hair free. 'I'm here out of nosiness,' she said unashamedly, following Kate through to the kitchen where she watched her open her box, 'and to bring Kate a prezzie from the female staff…'

'Now, these are quite something.' Guy stepped forward to inspect the six long-stemmed glasses Kate was setting out.

'They are, and thank you so much, Sue… Thank you all so much,' Kate enthused, genuinely pleased.

'There's a card there…' Sue pointed it out '…signed by all of us.'

'What a pity I didn't bring a bottle.' Guy said. 'We could have christened the glasses.'

'Or wet the house roof,' riposted Sue, giving a little start, as Kate did, when the doorbell shrilled yet again.

It was Mike on the step this time, a bag at his feet, a rolled-up duvet under one arm and a bottle in his free hand. Behind him a taxi reversed down the drive. Kate stared in astonishment. 'But, Mike, I was coming to fetch you this evening…to the dance. I didn't think—'

'Couldn't wait,' he said, bending to kiss her cheek. 'I've not seen you for a week, and I thought I could help with some of the odd jobs. I'm not bad at do-it-yourself, remember?' He broke off as he saw Guy and Sue. 'Oh, you've already got company. Sorry if—'

'Like the Greeks, we came, bearing gifts,' Guy said drily. Sue crossed to Mike's side, exclaiming when he unwrapped his gift—a bottle of sparkling wine.

'Well, here are the glasses and here is the wine—now we really *can* toast the house.' Kate tried her best to sound welcoming and not show how she felt about Sue and then Mike, arriving unexpectedly.

When the wine had been drunk and enjoyed she took Sue on a tour of the house. Mike stayed downstairs with Guy as he'd seen it before on a brief recce with Kate when the purchase was going through. 'It's absolutely ace!' Sue oohed and aahed in every one of the rooms.

'So useful to have a few bits and bobs of furniture left as well. I expect you and Mike are staying here tonight—after the dance, I mean?' They were back downstairs when she said this, but before Kate could reply Mike did so, turning from the sink where he was rinsing the glasses. 'No, actually not,' he said. 'I'll be here on my own. Kate doesn't want to leave her mother all night so soon after the burglary.'

Kate blinked a little, not particularly pleased at the inference behind Mike's words—that but for the burglary and her mother's nervousness they would have been together tonight, curled up under that *gross* duvet. She glared at it down on the floor.

She looked at Guy's back. He was fiddling with the boiler again. 'Actually,' she said, 'I don't mean to stay here at all until I move in for good.'

It was Sue's turn to blink. 'Oh, well...right,' she said. She dragged her woolly cap down to eyebrow level and said she must be off. 'I've left the kids with Iris. She's having them tonight as well so I must go home and do my stint. I can drop you off at Larchwood on the way, if you like, Guy. You may have noticed that I had a mere thimbleful to drink so you'll be perfectly safe.'

'A lift would be just the job, Sue, thanks. We'll leave these two to their DIY and cleaning operations. See you tonight,' he said, smiling at them both in the doorway as he followed Sue down the path.

CHAPTER TEN

As a fund-raising event the Christmas dance had been a great success and, as Mike put it when Kate was driving him back to Mayfield Cottage, the organisers deserved a pat on the back.

'It was too crowded for comfort,' Kate said, her eyes on the road. It had rained earlier and then frozen, and she was wary of black ice. Uncharitably she was thinking that Mike could have offered to walk the short distance from the assembly rooms and save her this extra trip. She was tired from so much dancing and hoarse from trying to talk to countless people and partners against a level of noise that had to be a danger to eardrums, not to mention vocal cords.

The highlight, or highlights, of her evening had been her four dances with Guy, the last one a slow smoochy number. Their bodies had moved in a sinuous rhythm which had been almost unbearable. Towards the end of the evening she had missed seeing him, then Sue, spinning by with a partner from the Grainger practice, had told her he'd been called out. He hadn't returned, Kate had noticed. When Mike—not his usual sober self—had suggested they made a move themselves she had been only too glad to agree.

'Shame Guy was called out,' Mike said, breaking into her thoughts.

'He was the one on call...' Kate cornered carefully '...and Sue was all right, dancing like a dervish. She's got more get up and go than me.'

'I like Sue.'

'Most people do.' Guy amongst them. Kate flinched

150

from the memory of Guy kissing Sue in one of those crazy forfeit dances, her lithe shape in its green dress bending like a sapling bough.

They reached the cottage at last. Kate braked carefully, hearing Mike say as his hand found her thigh, 'But I like you best.'

'Good!' Kate laughed. Alcohol had stripped years off Mike's age. His comment and his darting, inaccurate kiss were those of a youth of sixteen. She returned his kiss, lips only, putting his hand back where it belonged. 'Hadn't you better go in?' she asked when he still sat there, staring at her, half his head in shadow from the strong moonlight so he seemed to be cast in stone.

He sighed. 'Course… Yes.' She saw his hand go out to the doorcatch, then he turned and grasped her arm. 'Kate, don't go, don't go home—spend the night with me! You could ring your mother, make the roads an excuse… I wouldn't…I won't pressure you into doing anything you don't want. I just want to have you beside me all night. I want to hold you in my arms. Please, Kate, please stay. It's not very much to ask!'

On the face of it, it wasn't—she knew that. Kate also knew that Mike, having given his word, would keep it. He wasn't a sex maniac, but the plain fact was she didn't want to stay with him. The thought of it neither repelled her nor appealed to her, but she'd had hours of Mike today…ever since just before midday when he'd arrived with his sparkling wine! Hysterical laughter rose in her throat. She coughed and quickly said, 'No, best to stick to what we arranged. Truly, Mike, it's best. I'll be along bright and early in the morning and take you home to breakfast.'

He sat still and upright, not looking at her now, or making any move to go. Not liking to switch on the engine and hurry him, she tensed behind the wheel and jumped when a car with a blaring hooter passed by at reckless speed. 'You can't stick my company for long—that's the crux of it, isn't it? I'm not disappointed, I expected you to say no.' He gave a short puffing laugh. 'Well, I'm not staying here on my own.' He began to get out of the car. 'I'll collect my gear, ring for a taxi and get off home.'

'You don't have to do that... There's no need for that!' Kate made to follow him, then thought better of it and stayed where she was. If he felt like that he could go. In a way she could understand his reaction. She stayed where she was till he emerged from the house, bag in hand, the cumbersome duvet under one arm, unrolling itself as he walked. She got out to help him and stand with him on the verge.

'You'll get cold,' he told her. 'You don't need to wait—the cab will be here in five minutes.' Even as he spoke it turned the corner, bathing them in light. He turned to her briefly. 'I'll ring you. Asterleigh Park,' he said to the driver, who was leaning back to open the rear door.

The taxi turned, using Kate's drive, and then they were off, Mike a thin blur in the back, the hump of the duvet swaying beside him like an extra passenger.

'I thought,' Laura said at breakfast next morning, 'that you were going over to fetch Mike.'

'That was the arrangement, but Mike changed it. He went straight home last night.'

'You mean, back to his flat in Asterleigh Park?'

At Kate's brief nod, Laura continued to sip her tea, not unduly surprised. Kate's next remark, however, claimed her full attention.

'I'm going to have to tell him I can't go back to living with him, Mummy...or marry him...or anything.' Kate hadn't slept much all night.

'Oh, darling, are you sure?'

'I thought you'd be pleased. Yes, I'm quite sure. Last night was a sort of turning point, I think, or the whole of yesterday was. I felt as though I was being rushed downhill into something I didn't want. The thing is, I've changed. I didn't realise how much until Mike came back again—from America, I mean.' Kate stopped trying to eat. The smell of toast sickened her.

'You've not changed,' Laura said. 'You've moved on, which isn't quite the same.'

I've moved towards Guy, Kate thought. I'm in love with him. I really love him. She avoided her mother's eye. She was about to say something else, Kate could tell, and presently out it came.

'I've come to like Mike.' Laura's tone was firm. 'He's more thoughtful than he once was, but he's still…well, a bit immature. He needs a lot of propping up. He isn't positive enough for you, Kate.'

'I dread telling him.'

'Well, you're going to have to, and the sooner the better.'

'I'm still very fond of him. I still care about him.'

'I expect you do. No woman ever forgets her first lover,' Laura declared with feeling, so much feeling that for an astounded second Kate saw a new side to her mother.

Immediately after an early lunch, which the two of them had together, Kate drove to Asterleigh on roads that were tricky but thawing out rapidly. Mike's flat, which she had only seen once, was in one of those large modern blocks which seemed soulless and unfriendly. She got no reply to her ring, which didn't surprise her too much. He'd most likely gone out to lunch or taken the train to see Tom. His curtains were drawn back— she could see that from the road—so he wasn't ill or anything. It was frustrating to have rehearsed what she was going to say, then be faced with a tight-shut front door. She would have to come over tomorrow after evening surgery.

Of course, there was always the possibility, and this occurred to her on the way home, that after last night's fiasco Mike would end things himself. Perhaps he'd ring her this evening or even write—he hated confrontations, she knew. If it happened like that it would save his pride and she'd feel better about it. The last thing I want is a row, she thought. I think too much of him for that.

When Kate got to Larchwood next morning Sue was getting ready for her clinic, putting a clean roll of sheet on the couch and setting up her trolley. 'Have a good time on Saturday?' she asked, clinking forceps into a dish.

'I did, yes.' Kate paused in the doorway, clutching a fistful of mail.

'Saw you in the small hours, saying goodnight to Mike, but why do it outside in the car when you've got a comfortable house a mere garden path away?' Sue was pulling her leg, but she was also curious. She really wanted to know—not that Kate intended explaining.

'So, where were you, behind the hedge?' she retorted, moving on.

'Driving by with Oliver Race, who took me home. He hooted but neither of you stirred. Lost to the world, no doubt!'

'At the risk of disturbing girlish confidences, may I have a word, please, Kate?' This was Guy, calling out from his room. Sue pulled a face as Kate made her way towards the voice, wishing Guy's door had been shut.

He looked as he always did in the morning, well groomed and doctorish, sitting there in her uncle's chair. A shaft of sunlight sliced over his head and shoulder, catching his arm as he passed a buff envelope of case notes across the desk. 'As Helen Stanhope is one of yours, over to you,' he said, just as Kate caught sight of the little girl's name on the front.

'Is she coming in? Has her voice come back?' Kate hoped this was the case, but Guy was already shaking his head.

'She's in the General, seriously ill. I got her admitted on Saturday night. She'd apparently been sick and in pain all day. She went straight up to Theatre from Casualty, where surgery revealed…confirmed my worst fears…that her appendix had ruptured and peritonitis was already widespread.'

'Oh, no! How is she now?' Kate rapped out the words.

'Hyperpyrexic, has two drains *in situ*, being nursed in the sitting position, drugs going in via the IV line, nil by mouth. I rang ten minutes ago. Mrs Stanhope is with her constantly—slept there last night. Her husband was away on business in the North, but came back yesterday. I went in, too, just for a minute or two.'

'I wish you'd let me know. I'd have gone—she *is* my patient!' Kate sounded accusing, without meaning to. Guy's brows rose the merest fraction.

'I didn't want to spoil your weekend. I assumed you'd be busy at the house.'

'I wasn't, and I wish you'd rung me. I suppose,' Kate went on, 'that Nell was the reason you were called away from the dance.'

'She was, and if only I'd been called sooner…like during the morning. Whatever possessed Mrs Stanhope to wait so long when the child was in so much distress, I just don't know. If Nell had been opened up twelve hours earlier the abscess would have been caught before it burst.'

'I've no doubt she's blaming herself now, poor Ann!' Kate couldn't help sympathising. 'I dare say, with Nell being unable to make any sound, it wasn't that simple for a lay person to tell how ill she was. Nell is prone to bilious attacks. I expect Ann thought it was that. She's a nervous child. Anyway,' she finished, 'I'll go in and see her myself after I've done my house calls, just for a minute or two.'

'I thought you might. So, over to you?'

'Yes,' Gathering up her things, Kate went thoughtfully out of the room and into her own. She sat at her desk for a minute or two, still deep in thought. Peritonitis, as well she knew, was a potential killer, especially the generalised sort, even when tackled by modern drugs. Poor little Nell. And poor Ann and Don Stanhope. They must be going through hell. They'd had such bad luck lately, first the grandfather and now this.

A thump and a bang, which was the sound of the street door, opening and shutting, followed by a mumble of voices from the waiting-room, heralded the first patients and alerted Kate to the fact that her list was good and long. After the usual spate of coughs, colds and flu complainers, followed by two rheumatic patients and a girl with conjunctivitis, a middle-aged woman whom Kate hadn't seen before came in and sat down. She was plump and tightly buttoned into a checked overcoat, with a felt hat like an old-fashioned policeman's helmet rammed down straight.

'How can I help you, Mrs Boulter?' Kate smiled at her encouragingly, trying to meet her eyes under the brim of her hat.

'It seems a silly thing to come and see you about, Doctor.' She was a very diffident lady. 'I've been having pain in my fingers. It's there most of the time, but especially bad at night...in bed, I mean. It wakes me up. It's this hand, my right one.' She laid it on the desk.

'Any loss of sensation? Do you drop things?'

'Quite often, yes.'

'Tell me exactly where the pain comes.' Kate turned her patient's hand palm uppermost.

'It passes up the middle finger. I get tingling in my fingers, just in the tips, but the pain in the middle finger is the worst. I don't want to seem to be making a fuss but it's sometimes excruciating, it really is.'

'I believe you, and you're not making a fuss.' Kate examined her hand. 'You say,' she went on, 'that you sometimes drop things so do you get pain in your thumb and index finger as well?'

'Yes, and when it's really bad it goes up into my arm.'

'Not pleasant.' Kate jotted down these details in Mrs Boulter's notes. 'Your pain,' she told her patient, 'is due to pressure on a nerve. It's the nerve that runs along the front of your wrist underneath a ligament. There's a tunnel between the ligament and bones of the wrist, containing the tendons that work your hand. When this tunnel becomes narrowed, perhaps through arthritis, the nerve is compressed and gives rise to pain...considerable pain. What you're suffering from is what is called carpal tunnel syndrome.'

'Can it be cured or relieved? How do I get rid of it? I do have arthritis, I know.'

'Yes, so I see.' Kate looked back in her notes. 'The pain,' she went on, 'can be relieved by injection, and I can do this now, if you like. It's an uncomfortable procedure as the needle has to go deep in your wrist into the tunnel itself. It won't be the quick prick of a flu jab, and you'll need to hold very still.'

'Oh, go ahead, Doctor. Please do it!' Mrs Boulter shrugged out of her coat, thrust up the sleeve of a cardigan and blouse, and laid her arm on the desk.

Reaching into her cupboard for a phial of cortisone and a disposable syringe, Kate drew up the drug. Taking the patient's hand onto her knee, she ascertained the exact spot and, as gently as she could, pushed the needle in. Mrs Boulter groaned deep in her throat, and immediately apologised.

'No need, you were great. All done now.' Kate disposed of the syringe. 'Now, what I suggest you do is see how you go, then come back and see me at the end of February, when you may need another injection. You should be pain-free until then and able to sleep at night.'

'My husband will be delighted. He does love his night's sleep but when I'm awake so is he, which doesn't exactly make for a trouble-free married life.' Mrs Boulter laughed.

She was nice, Kate thought, amusing, too, but why did she wear such hideous clothes? Plump or not, she was attractive under that awful hat and coat. She was also brave. Kate wished she was. She was dreading having to explain to Mike, who had made no move to contact her. She would have to see him tonight. But she couldn't think about that now, she told herself, ringing for her very last patient—a Mr Cartwright with a rash on his back. After he'd been examined and sent off with a prescription for neomycin, Kate dealt with her mail, gave instructions to Janice and set off on her calls. She had six to make and it was a quarter to one before she got to the General Hospital and over to the children's wing.

Nell was in a six-bedded surgical ward. Kate could see her from the doors but before she went in she had a word with the ward sister, who told her she was slightly better. 'There's no dyspnoea, she's less febrile, blood pressure's stable. Once Mr Maxwell has seen her again, which will be this afternoon, I'm hoping we may be able to dispense with the nasogastric tube. She'll not be feeling very chipper, though, till her wound drains are out. Perhaps you could do something with the mother, Doctor. She persists in blaming herself.'

Ann Stanhope, who was sitting by Nell's bed, was indeed blaming herself. 'It just never occurred to me, Doctor, that it wasn't one of her bilious attacks. She gets pain with those and I didn't think it was anything worse till she started to roll about the bed, drawing up her legs. And that was late on, past eleven at night...'

'You weren't to know, Ann, and things weren't normal, were they? I mean—' Kate strove to be as tactful as possible '—Nell couldn't speak or complain.'

'My common sense should have told me, and that's another thing—it'll be difficult for her in here, not being able to speak.'

'The nurses will know how to deal with that.' Nell was asleep, Kate saw. She had no intention of waking her for sleep was a healer. 'I'll be back tomorrow,' she promised, 'just for a little while to see how she is.'

Nell looked a pathetic scrap, lying there against a mountain of pillows, her face haggard. Fluid was running into one arm, a tube was taped to the side of her face and her legs were looped over a long pillow, like a bolster, to stop her from slipping down the bed. It was small wonder her mother was distressed. Kate felt quite moved herself.

As she left via Casualty's waiting hall, the nearest exit to the car park, Kate was surprised to see Guy, making his way in. 'I wondered if I'd see you.' He strode towards her, avoiding the queues at the desks. 'I've been to the labs to try to hurry up one or two blood results, and I thought I'd pop up and see the Stanhope girl while I'm here. How did you find her?'

'There's a definite improvement...' She gave him the details, ending, 'So as long as she doesn't relapse...'

'If her temp's down it means they've got the infection under control. Look...' He stepped aside to allow a man in a wheelchair to pass. 'I'm not going to be long. Hang on for me, can you? We could pop over the road and have a sandwich and a coffee—it's too late for a proper lunch. There's something I want to tell you.'

'Oh, is there? Nice or nasty?' Kate laughed, but felt

her mouth dry up...in fear, perhaps, or trepidation. It was probably something to do with his plans for when his locum stint ended, she thought.

'Well, for me it's exciting.' He looked mysterious.

So it *is* that, she thought, and I bet it's abroad again, most likely Africa. Her spirits plummeted as she said she'd wait for him.

Off he strode and she went to the payphones to let her mother know she wouldn't be home. Laura made no fuss, she never did, but she chatted for a bit. Kate only half listened, as she scanned the crowd, anxious not to miss Guy. Then she saw someone else—a slightly built man with light brown hair and an anorak to match, coming towards the line of phones, and she felt her jaw go slack.

Good Lord, it was Tom...Tom from Fulham...but what was he doing here? Why here and not the Redlands Clinic if it was Mike he wanted to see? Perhaps he'd come to see *her* but why here, why the hospital? Why not ring her at Larchwood? And then suddenly she knew, suddenly she guessed. An icy finger seemed to make its way down her spine from neck to waist... *Something had happened to Mike!*

She shouted goodbye to her mother and slammed down the receiver. She walked towards Tom who saw her and was at her side in seconds. 'Kate!' His arms went round her in a convulsive, nervous hug. 'I was just about to ring you. What luck to find you here!' He looked upset, untidy, his hair awry and his eyes staring straight into hers.

'Why are you here? What's happened? Tell me!' Kate gripped his sleeve. 'It's Mike, isn't it? Something's happened.'

'Yes, I'm afraid so.' Tom led her to the chairs. 'He had an accident—a road accident—on Saturday night or early Sunday morning. It was just outside Melbridge. He was in a taxi that skidded and overturned. He's here, upstairs in Abbot Ward…head injury.' Tom was looking upset. 'The driver, who escaped injury, radioed for help. Mike was brought in here early on Sunday. The awkward thing was—'

'How is he now? How bad is he?' Kate's head reeled. The dance and her refusal to stay the night with him…the taxi and those terrible roads…

'He's concussed, there's no skull fracture, and he came to—so they told me—early yesterday, but he was confused. He still is—talks at random then goes to sleep again. He had no identification on him, and there was nothing in his wallet, but a few notes, one of my business cards and a snapshot of you. The police came to the shop this morning and I drove down straight away. It was a shock, still is. I've rung his parents and notified Redlands Clinic—he'd want me to do that. I was just on the point of coming to see you when there you were, here you are!' Tom gave a twisted smile.

'Oh, Tom!'

'He'll be all right, you know.' He took her hands in his.

'We'd been to a dance. Mike was on his way home…' Kate found she could hardly speak. 'I'm going up to see him now for myself! Are his parents coming down?'

'They are. They should be here about three. I've booked them in at The Bridge.'

'You've done a lot. You've been fantastic, Tom!' As Kate lurched to her feet she backed into Guy, who'd come up behind them and was looking at Tom in a puzzled way and at Kate with alarm. Quickly she explained.

'Guy, this is Tom Baker. Mike's had an accident. He's in Abbot Ward. I'm going there. Tom will tell you about it!' She darted off and left them there, managing to catch a lift on the point of closing its doors.

Abbot Ward—the neuro ward—was a long way from

the children's wing, and even when Kate had reached the right floor there was still a fair distance to cover. The entrance to the ward was guarded by a zealous young student nurse, who was adamant that she couldn't go in.

'He's concussed, which means that the functions of his brain are temporarily disturbed,' she explained, as though she was quoting from one of her textbooks, causing Kate, in her shocked state, to very nearly explode.

'I know what concussed means, Nurse. What I'd *like* to know is how he is now, if he's awake and why I can't go in!'

Hearing raised voices, Sister appeared and took Kate, whom she knew by sight, down the corridor into her office. It was from her Kate learned that Mike's concussion was in the moderate category.

'An EEG done yesterday showed few abnormal waves. At the moment when he wakes he talks at random and has no awareness of his surroundings, but there's no bony injury. All he needs now is rest and quiet. Still, come in and take a peep at him—not that he's a pretty sight.'

This was said, Kate knew, to prepare her for the fact that Mike looked as though his head had been kicked around like a ball. There he lay, sleeping and helpless, a single pillow under his neck, a pad and bandage covering a wound at his temple. His face was contused and swollen and black especially beneath his eyes, his fair lashes appearing white against the darkened skin.

Kate was totally silent, bereft of words. It was all she could do to stand upright and manage to breathe. It wasn't until she was back in the corridor that she was able to say she would return for evening visiting. 'I expect his parents will be here then.'

Downstairs she found Guy with a plate of sandwiches and two plastic beakers of tea on a chair beside him. 'Your friend, Tom, has gone to the hotel to wait for

Mike's parents,' he said. 'He's booked them in there for a couple of nights.'

'You shouldn't have waited.' She was glad to see him, but couldn't help sounding terse. It was necessary to hold herself together and not dissolve into tears. 'And I'm not hungry,' she added.

'I thought you'd say that, but I am, and I hate eating alone. There's no time to go across the road, is there, so please me by having a go?'

She drank the tea first, which was surprisingly hot and reviving. Even the sandwiches—some sort of salad between blotting-paper slices of bread—were acceptable and filling. 'Thank you for waiting,' she said.

'Any time.' He noted her returning colour with satisfaction.

'Mike looks dreadful.'

'I expect he does.' There was a pause and then Guy went on, 'But, as you and I know, faces with so much soft tissue bruise dramatically.'

'Tom will have told you about the taxi, skidding.' Kate's remark was more statement than question, and she saw Guy nod.

'He did, and from that I concluded Mike had a sudden yearning for home.'

'I upset him over a…over a trifle.' Kate decided not to explain—not in full, that was. It didn't seem fair. All she said was, 'Even so, he didn't have to go. I didn't want him to.'

'Oh, dear. I see.' Guy was making guesses based partly on what Tom Baker had told him a few minutes previously. 'I just hope,' he went on, 'that you haven't caught Mrs Stanhope's disease and are blaming yourself.'

'I have all the symptoms!' Kate managed to smile against the pricking of tears. This seemed to be a good

point at which to get off the subject of Mike so she asked
him how he had found Nell when he'd been upstairs.

'Well, there's an improvement, isn't there?' He took
her cup and placed it with his on the chair. 'If she can
keep it up and the drugs do their work, she'll be able to
get rid of that feeding tube and, possibly, one of her
drains. No one feels on top of the world when they're
threaded through with tubes. Now, Kate—' his tone al-
tered '—to business! How would you like me to take
your evening surgery? John would come through and
take charge of mine—he's only waiting for the chance!
You see, I'm sure you'll want—'

'No, Guy, I won't. No.' She shook her head. 'I'd
rather not alter—upset—things. I shall be coming back
here, of course, to see Mike, but evening visiting is from
half past six to eight, which will fit in perfectly.'

'And what about your calls?'

'I'm just about to begin on them. Thank heaven for
ice-free roads!' She rose and reached for the tab of her
zip, sliding it up to her chin. 'Thanks for the tea and
sympathy—both appreciated.'

He got up beside her. 'You didn't,' he said, 'allow
me to sympathise.'

'I was glad you were here.' She smiled up at him and
met his downward gaze, feeling the pressure of his hand
on her shoulder, just as Ann Stanhope stepped out of the
nearest lift, waved and began to come over.

'I'm sure it's you she wants to see.' Kate waved back
to her, but retreated quickly, slipping through the exit
doors.

CHAPTER ELEVEN

MIKE'S condition remained much the same while his parents, the mild-mannered Mr and Mrs Merrow, sat by him that afternoon. They had gone back to The Bridge Hotel when Kate arrived at the hospital shortly before seven o'clock. Tom was with Mike but was relieved to see Kate because he was anxious to get home. 'I'll need to open the shop tomorrow, Kate, and there are a dozen things to be seen to.' He looked apologetic as he said this, and Kate was quick to reassure him.

'Tom, you've been fantastic and, of course, you must go home. You've done so much.'

'The worst was calming the Merrows down. They idolise Mike, as you know.' Kate did know, but lone offspring were often idolised, especially when they came late in life, and Mike was the child of elderly parents. They had left a message with Tom, asking Kate to have dinner with them, which she was going to do.

'So it looks as though I'll be carrying on your good work,' Kate said, and said goodbye to him in the ward corridor, before going into see Mike, who was having one of his awake periods. Would he know her or not?

She sat, drawing her chair close against the bed. She spoke to him quietly, but he was talking gibberish—jerked-out phrases like 'no good', 'can't manage', 'not right', and 'too hard'. His eyes were on her face and she tried to take his hand, but he resisted her touch, thrusting his arm underneath the sheet.

When he dozed off yet again she left the hospital and drove the short distance to The Bridge Hotel for her date with Mike's parents, relieved that under her workaday anorak she was wearing a decent suit of soft blue wool that was very nearly knee-length. She had met the Merrows several times when she was living with Mike. They had liked her, she knew that, but they'd never come to terms with her and Mike's relationship at Mamesbury and had said so many times. It was, therefore, with some uneasiness that Kate parked the car in the near-empty space behind the hotel. Would they blame her for what had occurred?

There were Christmas trees flanking the wide entrance doors, and their coloured lights glowed in the semi-darkness, patterning the steps which she presently mounted, swallowing against a dry throat. She saw the Merrows as soon as she entered the foyer. They were through in the cocktail lounge, facing the doors and looking out for her.

Cedric Merrow, tall and thin and looking as Mike would at seventy, shot to his feet and came forward to greet her, shaking her by the hand, while his wife, Lilian, just as tall but voluptuous of build, folded Kate into a cushioned embrace. 'How lovely to see you, dear!'

They were drinking sherry, but ordered a tonic for Kate, which was all she wanted to drink. She was taking her first sip, and agreeing with Mr Merrow that the hotel decorations were tasteful, when across the room, facing her and raising his hand to her, she saw Guy with a sandy-haired, thickset man who was laughing at something he'd said.

'It's my step-cousin, Guy Shearer,' she told the Merrows as she waved back. 'He's doing a locum at Larchwood at the moment.'

'I think Mike has mentioned him at some time or other. Now, Kate,' Mrs Merrow went on, 'we'd like to have your professional view of Mike's condition. You see, Cedric and I wondered if something might have been missed, a clot, or something like that...'

'Or a hair fracture.' Mr Merrow coughed, putting down his glass. 'They don't always show up clearly on X-ray.' As a retired hospital administrator, he felt he knew about such things.

'I'm sure nothing's been missed,' Kate told them reassuringly. 'Concussion takes its time—even moderate concussion, which is what Mike has. It's distressing that he doesn't know us and, of course, he looks so awful, but another twenty-four hours will make a great difference all round. When I saw him just now I felt he *did* know me once or twice or was right on the edge of doing so—'

'Will there be memory loss?' Cedric Merrow interrupted. 'Will he, for instance, think you and he are still in Wiltshire, working locally?'

'As his period of unconsciousness was fairly short, that's unlikely,' Kate said. She was thinking, please God, please, not that, but knew all the same that retrograde amnesia was a possibility.

'Well, we shall stay here till he's well enough to come home with us. That new job of his will have to wait.' Lilian Merrow sounded, for her, quite fierce. 'We'll stay for as long as it takes.'

Kate was just saying that she was sure the Redlands Clinic would be sympathetic when, at a sign from the waiter, they went through to the restaurant. They were at the soup stage when she saw Guy and his companion leave the hotel, stopping in the foyer to collect their coats and pushing their way through the heavy revolving doors and disappearing into the night. Kate didn't know whether she felt relieved, bereft or a mixture of both, but the sensation of being alone that followed was horrid and she shivered as she sat.

'We're so glad you and Mike are together again,' she heard Mrs Merrow say. 'We do hope you'll get married this time. It'll settle him down, you see. If you'd been man and wife before, I'm sure Mike would never have gone to America. When you refused him it broke his heart. He wrote and told us so.'

Kate had finished her soup, which was just as well or she was sure she'd have choked. As it was, it was all she could do to hold her tongue and not tell the concerned and accusatory couple in front of her that their son had never ever proposed, not in actual words. Oh, he'd hinted at marriage in a sometime/someday kind of way, to which she'd responded with enthusiasm. Mike had *known* she would have married him.

'It took great courage on his part to come back and approach you again. Mike's easily put down, easily hurt—rather like me in a way.' Mrs Merrow tried the effect of a smile, while Kate sat, stony-faced.

'I think we should leave Mike and Kate to sort things out for themselves.' Cedric Merrow could feel Kate's tension stretching to meet his own.

'The main thing now is for Mike to get well. Nothing can be sorted out till then.' Kate stared unseeingly down at her plate of grilled plaice, which the assiduous waiter had just put in front of her. 'I'd like to say, though—' and now she was looking Mrs Merrow straight in the eye '—that I've never knowingly hurt Mike, and I hope I never will.'

'Thank you, dear.' Not entirely convinced, Mrs Merrow began to eat, and the meal continued without further reference to Mike and his sufferings. They talked, instead, of Cedric's gardening successes, of the prizes he'd won at shows and of the holiday he and Lilian were hoping to have on Madeira next year. However, it was thin-ice stuff, and not holding well, and Kate was relieved when their pudding was ordered and eaten, and she could talk of getting home.

'No, I won't stay for coffee, thank you,' she said. 'I

ought to be going now. I've got an early start again tomorrow. A doctor's work is never done!'

'Oh, my dear, I'm sure it *isn't*!' Mrs Merrow took her literally. It was Cedric who escorted her to the doors, saying goodnight with a papery kiss and a squeeze of her arm, which Kate thought might be a mute apology for Lilian's earlier remarks about her and Mike.

It was enlightening, though, what she had said, Kate thought as she drove home, for it showed Mike up as a liar as well as a cheat. He'd lied to his parents about cheating on her to make his own case look better. This surprised her more than saddened her. She would never have thought it of him. 'You've learned a salutary lesson, Kate Burnett,' she muttered to herself as she turned into the drive at Riverstone, thankful to be home.

When she telephoned the hospital at breakfast-time next morning to ask how Mike was, she was informed that, although complaining of headache, he was aware of his surroundings and beginning to take things in. He also— and Kate knew this was an important sign—remembered the accident.

She told Guy about it when she got to Larchwood, going into his room where he was slitting envelopes open with his vicious-looking paperknife.

'Looks as though he'll come out of it none the worse for wear,' he said, glancing briefly at her then down at his papers again.

'I thought I'd go in this evening and leave the afternoon free for his parents. They're staying on at The Bridge, possibly till the end of the week.'

'They're the couple you were with last night, I expect? I liked the look of them,' he added before she had time to answer.

'Mike's like his father,' she said.

'I could see the resemblance.' Guy turned to face her,

swinging in the swivel chair. 'The man *I* was with,' he told her, 'was Alex Crighton, one of the GPs from Barham Health Centre. He wants me to join his firm. I was over there last week, meeting the other two partners and seeing over the centre. It's the kind of set-up that attracts me, with every facility under one roof—diagnostic equipment, a small theatre, a laboratory section, half a dozen treatment rooms, a dispensary and a physiotherapy room. Four separate practices are housed there—the area they serve is huge. If the local medical committee approves of me, that's where I shall be!'

'Good heavens, Guy!' Kate sat there, trying to take it in. 'So you won't go abroad?'

He shook his head. 'Oh, congratulations,' she said. What she wanted to do was jump up and throw her arms round his neck, but something about his expression and manner kept her in her seat. 'I bet Uncle John and Sylvia are pleased.'

'Delighted.' He swung himself back to face the desk again. 'But until all the red tape's out of the way I don't want anyone, other than family, told.'

'No, course not.'

'Sue knows, but I've sworn her to secrecy.'

Kate said nothing to that, for his words had taken her aback. He'd told Sue *and before her.* Surely that meant—could only mean—that the two of them were close, closer than she'd thought, anyway. Somehow she managed to make one or two more congratulatory noises before she escaped to her room. She had no time to close the door completely, however, before it was pushed open again by Guy. He leaned in with his hand on the knob.

'I forgot to mention that after this evening's surgery I'm off to Town for three days to see Pa and Jean. John will slot back into his rightful place until Monday. He says he can't wait. All in all, he'll be glad to see the back of me for good, I think.'

'Will you live over at Barham?' Kate's voice was small.

'Sure thing, yes. Six miles is a bit too far to go to and fro, especially at night.'

Just beyond him, over his arm, Kate could see Sue, taking her first patient through into the treatment room. Other patients, for herself and Guy, were filing in at the doors. 'Looks like duty calls,' she said prosaically. 'Enjoy your few days in Town.'

'Can't wait,' she heard him say as he went back into his room. Then came the drone of his buzzer as he summoned in a young man on crutches. The long day had begun.

On Wednesday Dr John told Kate that Guy had been head-hunted by the Grainger Practice. 'Bob Grainger's retiring at the end of March. The partners very much wanted him to join their team.'

'But he decided on Crightons and the health centre.' Kate was trying to sound not *too* interested, but didn't quite manage it.

'I don't think it was a difficult choice.' John gave her a searching look. 'He felt, as I do, that to join Graingers would, in a sense, be joining a rival firm...not that we're rivals, exactly, but we *are* territorially close, and there could have been difficulties.'

'Six miles is just a nice distance away,' Kate said, and her uncle laughed.

Later, as she set off on her calls, she made herself stop thinking about Guy and reflected instead on yesterday when the Merrows, despite having seen Mike in the afternoon, had appeared at his bedside again during the evening when Kate had been there. It was annoying because she and Mike could have talked together as Mike was now well enough to do so. 'He's a fit young man with a good thick skull,' Sister had told the Merrows.

While they'd still been talking to her Mike had asked

Kate to go in today. 'Mid-afternoon, if you can manage it,' he'd said. 'Mother and Dad will be having a nap at the hotel then. Please try to make it unless you've got something life-and-death on.'

She had promised she would and now as she drove along the town side of the river on her way to a patient who lived in an old-type bungalow on stilts she wondered how he'd react when she told him they could never be other than friends. I don't love him. It's all gone, drained away to the very last drop. He isn't the person I thought he was. Fondness is all there is. I certainly don't want to set him back, though, or hurt him in any way.

The bungalow, which she presently climbed up to via precarious wooden steps, was small enough to be a tree house but it was comfortable enough inside. The elderly Mrs Pritchard, who lived there with her ancient tabby cat, was sitting by an open fire, toasting bread on a fork. She had a dry, irritating cough and, knowing of her difficulty in getting to a chemist, Kate had brought her a bottle of cough mixture.

'Two teaspoonfuls four-hourly, Mrs Pritchard, and if you're not better in a week ring me at the surgery and I'll come out again.'

She was offered tea and toast, but politely declined. 'I have my tea at home before I start evening surgery…' she smiled '…and this afternoon I'm seeing a friend in hospital.'

Mrs Pritchard didn't mind. 'Then I mustn't keep you,' she said. She waved Kate off from her sitting-room window, watching her start up the car.

Kate drove straight to the hospital. She turned into the wide entrance sweep and carefully avoided a lorry, unloading fir trees outside Casualty. It was not long now until Christmas and, perhaps inevitably, her mind went back to her training days—to her year's hospital stint when she'd helped with the decorations and joined in the singing on Christmas Eve. She and Mike had just moved into the flat at Mamesbury. She had filled a stocking for him, and he'd given her a necklace of lapis lazuli.

She felt hollow inside and her stomach rolled as she took the lift up to the neuro floor and walked along the passage to his ward. He was looking out for her. His face still battered, a pad and plaster still adorning his temple, but he was smiling and looked alert. 'Headache gone?' Kate asked him.

'Bar a twinge or two. I expect to be discharged tomorrow after my consultant's been round, but not home—to Redlands,' he said to her surprise. 'My boss visited late last night. My job's all right, and they want me to convalesce at the clinic for as long as it takes. Now, how about that for a good offer?'

'They must think a lot of you, Mike, but what about your parents?'

'Oh, they'll go home, obviously, once I'm out of here. I couldn't cope with a long car journey at the moment.'

'No, I don't suppose so.' Kate moistened dry lips, nerving herself to say what she knew she must, but as she framed the words Mike started to speak again.

'That taxi driver has been in, too. He seemed quite upset when he saw me. You know, Kate…' Mike moved forward from his pillows '…in those few terrifying seconds when I could feel the cab turning over, all I could think of was that I wanted to live…that if I escaped with my life I'd not ask for anything else *ever*. I practically made a pledge!'

Kate was aghast. 'Mike, how terrible!'

'No, no, you're missing the point.' He leaned back again, as though wearied. 'What I'm trying to say is that if you're trying to say we must split up I'm unlikely to go out and hang myself. I shan't like it, but I'll be all right.'

Kate could feel her heart turning over in hot, slow thumps. 'I'm sorry, Mike, but, yes, that's it. I've changed and I can't go back. I tried because I couldn't believe it at first, but as we went on seeing one another…'

'You knew it for sure?'

'Yes, I did.'

'I expected it.' His mouth thinned momentarily. 'Even so, it's a blow. Still, I'm not sorry I've come to Thames-side. I've got the kind of job I want. I may even fall in love again one day.' He looked carefully at her.

'We can be friends, I hope?' she ventured, and he laughed.

'I knew you'd say that. It's the classic come-back, isn't it? Actually, I'm sorry for Mum and Dad. They'd have liked you for a daughter-in-law.'

She felt goaded now, just enough to say, 'Well, don't let them blame me too much *this time round*!' Mike didn't answer, and she had no means of telling whether her shot had gone home because his discoloured face hid any blush of shame. Suddenly contrite, she reached for his hand, which grasped hers tightly.

'OK,' he said in a thick-sounding voice. 'OK, Kate, friends it is!'

Kate scarcely knew how she felt when she left the hospital some ten minutes later and drove home in the gathering dusk. She was relieved in part, she acknowledged that, but there was a sense of loss as well… No regrets, though, no repinings, no wondering if she'd done the right thing.

Laura had the sense and tact not to say very much that evening, except to reassure Kate that Mike would be all right. 'He'll find his own level one day, fall in love again as you will…if you haven't already.' She waited expectantly, but no comment was forthcoming from her daughter, whose face told her nothing at all.

*　　*　　*

'I would never have believed,' Dr John remarked after morning surgery next day, 'that I could have missed the toil and strife of practising medicine so much. Being back, seeing all the old faces...and bodies...plus some new ones as well has put me right back on target, Kate. I'm in my rightful place.'

'After Christmas it'll be "Burnett and Burnett" again.' Kate smiled at him over her desk. He had come in to see her about a new patient whom he thought should be on her list. 'When does Guy start with Crightons?' she asked.

'Mid-Feb,' her uncle supplied, 'but he's taking off from Christmas until then—going on holiday, which, of course, he richly deserves, bearing in mind that he came straight to us after the rigours of Africa.'

'Does he plan to go away for it?' Kate asked in a muffled voice.

'For part of it, yes, I think he does, but he'll probably house-hunt first. He's got to find somewhere to live at Barham. Talking of houses...' Her uncle removed his glasses and polished them, looking intently at Kate. 'Is your mother over that burglary business and settling down at Riverstone?'

'No, I don't think she is.' Kate looked troubled. 'She says the place doesn't feel the same. I know what she means but, to be honest, it hasn't affected me quite the same. Anyway, she's going to stay with a friend at Eltonhead for the weekend. I shall stay at Mayfield Cottage till she's back, taking Merle with me. I want to paper the spare bedroom so it'll be a good chance to do it.'

'And a good rehearsal for when you're living there on your own.' Her uncle looked at her quizzically, and she knew what was in his mind.

'I can see Mum's told you about Mike and me,' she said.

'We spoke on the phone last night and she told me. She and I have a habit of confiding in each other, Katie.' He rubbed the bridge of his nose. 'All I'll say is I think you're wise. It's very seldom that a broken-off relationship can jell again.'

Left alone at last, Kate began on her letters. She was crossing to the office later when Sue called out to her, asking how Mike was.

'Doing well. He'll probably be discharged tomorrow or Friday. Redlands are having him there to convalesce till he's fit to start work.'

'*Are* they?' Sue looked impressed. 'Well, all I can say is he must have made a mega-impression during his first week at work.'

'He's a first-rate physio.'

'I'll probably visit him there. I've a friend on the nursing staff, you know.'

'Yes, I think you mentioned it. Anyway, Sue, I must get on.' Kate walked further into the office. 'I want to visit young Nell Stanhope before I start my calls. Her voice has come back, would you believe, along with a really fantastic improvement in her condition? Apparently, she asked for a drink last night and actually vocalised!'

'Oh, I'm glad. She's such a nice little kid.' Sue's face softened.

'She is, and how are your two?'

'In full voice, praise be, and excited about Christmas.' It seemed to Kate that Sue was about to say something else, but there was a fair bit of noise in the office, with Meg on the phone and Janice busily typing, so perhaps she changed her mind because, wearing a faintly embarrassed expression, she went back to the treatment room.

Kate's waking thought on Saturday was that Guy would be back today. He had probably returned last night and was at Larchwood right at this moment. When I see him on Monday, do I tell him about Mike and me or not? she wondered. He may not be interested, and I can't just blurt it out. In any case, all he wants is a passing affair— a fun liaison. She thought of Sue, who was most likely colluding in that. He had told Sue about his new post. It was odd how much that rankled, seeming as it did to suggest a closeness other than a physical one.

It was seven-thirty and not yet light. From across the landing she could hear her mother moving about, packing her case for her weekend break at Eltonhead. Uncle John was on call until midnight on Sunday, which left Kate free to potter about at Mayfield Cottage and stay there overnight in the big furnished bedroom, overlooking the back. The thought of being there calmed her a little. She liked decorating, especially paper-hanging, and found it a kind of therapy. Getting out of bed and crossing to the bathroom, she told herself that things could be worse. 'It's count-your-blessings time, Kate,' she muttered. 'Perhaps once Guy has gone off to live at Barham you won't hanker quite so much.'

Four hours later she was in the Christmas shopping scrum in Morrisons', pushing through to the DIY section where she hoped to rent a steaming device to help strip the existing paper off her walls. This she was able to do without difficulty for not all that many people had their minds on wallpapering during the run-up to Christmas.

It was a mischievous fate that brought her back into the main shop again just in time to see Guy with Sue and her two little girls on the escalator on their way to Santa's grotto on the top floor. The younger girl was riding high atop Guy's shoulders. Sue was in red on the step above him, clinging tightly to her other child.

Up and up and up they went. Kate couldn't stop watching them and stood there till they reached the first floor, when more crowds hid them from view. What she felt as once more she started to move was shock but not surprise. There was a difference between the two states—it was shock that sent her out into the streets with a lump in her chest which was her heart, trying to beat.

Back at the car, which she'd had to leave on a meter in a side street, Merle greeted her warmly from the back seat, her long pink tongue hanging sideways out of her mouth. She barked as they drove off and out of the town to Fallerton Road, drawing up at the cottage at last.

It was warm inside for, acting on advice, Kate had kept the heating on. It had been on ever since Guy had lit the boiler last Saturday. Afterwards he'd kissed her, and then Sue had come... Sue, always Sue! There was something going on between Guy and her—that was probably why she hadn't mentioned him lately. At one time she'd never stopped going on about him and this morning there he'd been, out with her and her children, looking for all the world like a family unit, so perhaps it was serious.

'I can't think about it. I won't think about it. I'll keep busy and block it out.' Somehow it helped to say this out loud. It helped to keep angry too, for, yes, she was angry...with herself more than anyone for feeling so hurt and shut out.

Lunch first—canned meat for Merle. She tipped this out into a dish, ate her own biscuits and cheese and apple, then made her way upstairs. The rolls of new wallpaper were stacked in the cupboard on the landing. It was a walk-in cupboard, with the kind of door fastening that Mike had said was dangerous because if anyone was inside and it shut accidentally there was no way of getting out.

He had been going to replace it for her—he was particular about things like that. He had so many good points. What a pity she couldn't have stayed in love with him. How simple life would be if one could love to order, she thought.

Taking Merle in the bedroom with her, Kate let her lie on the bed while she applied steam to the walls and started stripping the paper. It came off with very little effort, strip after strip after strip. The little room fogged up like a sauna, making her eyelashes wet. The stooping and pulling, the bending and stretching, helped her state of mind. With only the fiddly bits to get off around the window, she decided to fetch a roll of paper to see how it would look.

Merle followed her out to the landing. She was bored, just lying around. She had her ball in her mouth and nosed it around, hoping for a game, but she got no joy from Kate who, deep in the cupboard, was struggling with the cellophane wrapping on the paper and breaking her fingernails. Why they had to wrap it so tightly she had no idea. Really, she was tired and ought to leave off as it was half past six.

'I'll go downstairs and have something to eat,' she said out loud, abandoning the paper and turning—just as the door slammed and she was plunged into darkness and instantaneous shock! It couldn't have happened... It *couldn't* have happened! She heard her own shout of, '*No*!' Then she heard the frantic sound of Merle, scrabbling on the outside of the door. 'You stupid dog, you stupid dog,' she shouted, for it was Merle who had done it—Merle who had blundered into the door.

Oh, why on earth hadn't she left her in the bedroom? What was she going to do? Kate thumped the door, slammed her hip against it and turned her back and kicked hard, but the wood was solid and firm. As the enormity of what had happened struck home, panic seared through her. Again she kicked and banged and thumped, and then she started to shout for help at the top of her voice. No one came. No one answered.

Quietness lay over the house, broken only by Merle, who snuffled under the door, making a keening noise.

Forcing herself to calm down, struggling for control, she sat on the floor and tried to think what to do. There was nothing in the cupboard but rolls of paper—no knife or file or saw which she could have slipped between the door and the jamb to try to force back the catch. Panic seized her again, blunting her brain and making her head spin. 'What shall I do? Oh, what shall I do?' she muttered to herself. She started to shout for help again but no one came. No one heard. Her prison was right at the centre of the house, and the house was detached, with all the windows tightly shut. No one would hear. No one would come looking for her either. Her mother was at Eltonhead. Her uncle knew she was here at the cottage, but he wasn't expecting her back until Monday morning for surgery.

I shall be here—she started to count on her fingers—for thirty-eight hours in the cold and the dark, without food or a lavatory. Oh, what shall I do? I can only shout. I must shout and shout at regular intervals...rest, then shout again.

Kate lost count of how many times she shouted and beat at the door. She sank down on her knees. Her voice had become hoarse with so much shouting and her throat felt harsh and raw. She was tired but straining to keep alert and small sounds seemed very loud—like her own breathing, her own heart beating, Merle's intermittent whine.

When the telephone rang in the hall she jumped up, then seethed with frustration at not being able to answer it. It rang and rang, then finally stopped. Even so, she dared to hope. Not many people knew her number here—only her mother, Uncle John and Mike. It was unlikely to be Mike—he wouldn't know she was here.

Oh, let it be Uncle John. He'll be worried at getting no answer so he'll come round here, I know he will.

She sat again, propped against the wall, silently praying. After a time—how long she had no idea—she heard the slam of a car door. Springing into action, she started to shout again. '*Here…here…here, I'm here.*' She banged and thrust at the door. The peal of the doorbell stopped her, and she listened. She heard a flapping sound, the rattle of the letterbox and then Guy's voice, floating through into the hall. Against Merle's crescendo of barking she could just make out the words, 'Keep still. Don't try to move. I'm breaking in!'

'Not hurt…shut in!' she shouted back. She heard nothing more, but it didn't matter. He was here, he'd come, he wouldn't go away. Guy, oh, Guy! The relief was so great that she burst into tears. She was still trying to stop when she heard him pounding up the stairs. Merle's barking stopped, the door was opened and she fell out over Guy's feet.

Kate heard him exclaim. She was dazzled by light—the light in the bedroom again. She found he had her locked against his side and they were sitting on the divan. There was the smell of the steamer and damp walls, the wool tang of his sweater. 'I thought, I thought…' She was trying to speak, but he told her to take her time.

'There's no rush. You're safe, you're out, you're free!' He dried her tears, stroked her hair and held her fast. Presently her body stopped its involuntary shuddering, and she felt herself calming down.

'I thought I was going to be in there till Monday. Merle barged into the door—there's a dangerous fastening. Mike was going to fix it, but then, of course…'

She felt Guy shift. 'Can you make it downstairs? It'll be warmer and you need something hot to drink.'

'Yes, I'm thirsty.'

He helped her downstairs and into the sitting-room,

where he made her lie on the big chesterfield, which was all the room contained. He stripped off his sweater and laid it over her, then went out into the kitchen. From where she lay she could hear him moving about, hear the sound of water splashing into the kettle and the chink of crockery. It was here, in this room, that they'd kissed so passionately exactly a week ago. It was a thought, a recollection, that should have kept her awake, but she was exhausted and the warmth of the fire, switched up to maximum, plus the comfort of his sweater, which smelled of him, was too much to fight against. By the time Guy returned with the tea Kate was fast asleep.

He didn't disturb her and she slept for an hour. She woke with a feeling of bewilderment, wondering where she was. Then Guy's head and shoulders swam into her vision. He was sitting on the floor, his back against the couch and his legs stretched out. His shirt looked pink in the glow from the fire. As she stirred he turned at once and pulled himself up to sit beside her as she swung her legs to the floor.

'Feeling better?'

'Yes, but how could I have slept...I mean, with you here?'

He laughed. 'I'm not sure how to take that!'

She shook herself awake, then looked at her watch and gave a yelp. 'Guy, it's *ten o'clock*! Don't you want to get back?'

'I'm staying the night,' he informed her. 'While you were asleep I rang John and told him what had happened to set his mind at rest. He was worried when I couldn't get you on the phone earlier—we thought you'd had an accident.'

'Of course...yes.' *Staying the night!* Kate began to feel dizzy again.

'I can sleep on this perfectly comfortably.' He gave the couch a slap.

'Well, if you're sure…' She couldn't meet his eyes.

'Never been more so,' he said cheerfully, and rose to turn down the fire.

'I'll get us some food.' Kate made for the door. To be busy would help. He was staying the night because of what had happened, because he was a caring type. Conscious of thirst as well as other yearnings, she drank glass after glass of water while Guy went to look in the cupboard and fridge, bringing out a tin of soup and some slices of York ham.

'I'll heat up the soup. There's plenty of bread if you want to make sandwiches.' She foraged in a drawer for a tin opener. She wasn't used to finding things in this kitchen, which still felt as if it belonged to the Rolfes, the previous owners.

'I'm not hungry, Kate, so nothing for me. I had a full meal before I came out.'

'And I only need soup.' How stilted they sounded— all this talk about food. She had her back to him as she heated the soup and heard him say, after a pause that seemed to her to go on for ever, 'It was during supper that John told me you and Mike had gone your separate ways.'

'Yes, but there was no unpleasantness.' Kate turned the gas down a notch. 'Mike just feels himself lucky not to have been killed last Saturday night.'

'What about you?'

'Me?' She turned, all but bumping into him. 'I'm relieved to be out of it, which sounds terrible, I know, but the sheer pressure of trying to get back to the way things were with us once was getting me down. I felt on edge and wasn't good company.'

All Guy said was, 'That's understandable.' He moved back to let her pass. 'Sit down and eat,' he added in a firm tone of voice, as though she were a child or a patient who needed feeding up.

She did as he'd said, and he sat on the opposite side of the table, drinking a cup of instant coffee and telling her about his day. 'I got back from Town around half-ten and had coffee with Ma and half a dozen coffee-morning ladies. John was out on a call. Then I collected Sue and the girls and took them to Morrisons' to see Santa Claus. A good time was had by all, after which I went to Barham to have lunch and look around the health centre. My appointment has been confirmed, by the way,' he finished with a smile.

'I didn't doubt that it would be.' Kate's face was expressionless. 'Are you and Sue having an affair?' she asked, with enough deliberate suddenness to knock him off balance. She had to know, and to ask, she reasoned, was the best way of finding out.

'I think you know I'm not,' he replied, not looking especially surprised. 'I like Sue. She has humour and guts, two qualities I admire. She likes to flirt and show off but she knows full well that we're not for one another. There's no spark to draw us close.'

'You told her about your appointment,' Kate said accusingly. The unspoken words, 'before you told me' hung in the air, and had an electric effect on an astounded Guy, who came around the table and drew Kate to her feet.

'Idiot girl…*darling* idiot!' He made her look at him. 'Sue got her information from Oliver—Oliver Race, Bob Grainger's partner. *He* knew about it because I turned down an offer from Graingers in favour of Crightons. Sue is currently seeing Oliver, giving him one of her whirls.'

'Oh.' Kate went limp with relief.

'Is that all you have to say?' His forefinger lifted her chin and he kissed her, softly at first, with no pressure as he whispered against her mouth, 'I thought you might say that you want me as much as I want you. I even thought you might say that you loved me, or were beginning to, anyway.'

'I do…I do!' The kiss deepened and they clung—then they broke apart. The journey upstairs was a race—so was getting out of their clothes. She was aroused as soon as their bodies touched. He was already there, yet he was gentle, ardent, careful of her. For seconds, only seconds, she felt a strangeness till his stroking, caressing hands made her cry his name and open herself to him, winding her legs round his back. She flew with him then, flew into country she'd known before, but this time it was different…different…different. Oh, the joy of spreading her wings…and soaring with him…and reaching the top…and floating down into peace.

'My wonderful Kate…my *perfect* girl!' He was still holding her close. She could feel the soft mat of his chest hair, tickling her face, feel the sweat on his arms, her own languidness.

'Love you…love you,' she murmured, and immediately fell asleep.

She woke at dawn to see the broad square of uncurtained window, outlining a grey December sky, which she viewed complacently. Guy was asleep, very nearly on his front, with an arm across her body. His face was turned into her neck and she had never been more comfortable. She slept again, and the next time she woke it was to the sound of chinking crockery. Guy, preceded by a tail-wagging Merle, was coming in with a breakfast tray. 'Is it for both of us?' She took it from him, discovering it was the lid of a box. She giggled when she saw it. 'What initiative!'

'My beautiful Kate—of course!'

She glowed, she felt beautiful, she adored him, she wanted to touch him all over. There he sat, damp from the shower, his naked, muscled torso rising from the band of his jeans, the dark stubble round his jaw lending a risqué, decadent look. She melted with love for him.

'I'm hoping,' he said, 'that from now on we'll be sharing everything.' He watched her start to pour the tea, her golden lashes downcast.

'You mean live together?' She was willing—she'd do anything he asked.

'If you like, yes, live together.' He took the cup she passed, then set it down on the floor and reached for her hand, his face hidden for a moment as he bent and kissed her palm. 'But what I want more than anything else is to marry you. Perhaps you don't feel you want to make that commitment?' His eyes looked straight into hers, love for her and anxiety intermixed, plain to see. She marvelled that he could doubt she wanted marriage with him more than anything else on earth.

'Oh, Guy.' She put the lid-tray on a chair. 'I *do* want to make that commitment! I love you, I want to marry you so *much*! I've loved you since Guy Fawkes's Night!'

'I've loved you since I first set eyes on you, but refused to acknowledge it.'

'All those years ago?'

'All five of them.'

'Oh, Guy!' She held out her arms, and once again they made love…and promises…and plans…and decisions… sure that the world was theirs.

Three hours later, when they set off for Larchwood, Guy got a bit bossy again. 'You must marry me,' he said, 'as soon as possible, and make an honest man of me!'

They were married at Melbridge Register Office three weeks later, with a full complement of relatives and friends on both sides. Afterwards they honeymooned on

Madeira—strongly recommended by Marcus Shearer and his new wife, Jean.

They were only away a week as there were several problems to be sorted out—the main one being where they would live so that both could travel, without too much hassle, to their respective surgeries. In the meantime, they lived at Mayfield, house-hunting at weekends and finding—as Guy said, by sheer luck—exactly what they wanted in the shape of an old rectory in the village of Upper Leigh, roughly midway between Melbridge and Barham.

Laura rented Mayfield Cottage from Kate. She had always liked it, she said. She had never felt the same about Riverstone after the burglary.

All in all, Uncle John declared, things couldn't have been better. They were all within shouting distance of one another—a proper family at last.

MILLS & BOON®

Makes any time special

Enjoy a romantic novel from Mills & Boon®

Presents™   Enchanted™   Temptation™

Historical Romance™   Medical Romance™